MW01601229

The Caretaker

Contents

Chapter 1

I stretched my arms over my head and pushed my chair back from the hotel table. Glancing at my phone, I could see it was midnight, the witching hour, and I was staying at South Dakota's most haunted hotel, the Alex Johnson, nestled in the hills of the badlands. A public relations company employed me for the state of South Dakota, and my current assignment was to investigate the hotels in the area that were rumored to be haunted. It was fun stuff, and while I didn't believe in such things, it was intriguing to write about and much better than covering local sweaty fairs.

I stood and crossed the room to my window overlooking Rapid City. It was quiet, with few cars about, and I raised my eyes to take in the surrounding landscape. Rolling black hills rose in the distance, with spiked edges of dark green against the sky's deep blue, and moonbeams showering the area in silvery light. It was a full moon tonight. *Wasn't that when all the crazies come out of the woodwork?* I thought. I huffed and glanced at my phone again. It was time to get to work.

I crossed the room and turned the handle slowly, careful not to make any noise, then stepped into the hall and repeated the process. It was silent in the darkened corridor, with all the guests safely slumbering in their rooms. I glanced at the number on my door: 812. According to legend, a new bride had thrown herself off the balcony in an apparent suicide, making this room the most haunted in the hotel, and now she now walked the halls as the Lady in White.

I wondered why it was always the 'Lady in White.' Why not red or yellow? Certainly not black, or no one would see her. I snorted and then froze as I heard a soft rustle and turned to look behind me. The hallway was empty. No Lady, no ghosts. I paced the carpeted floor, my feet noiseless as I walked. I could hear contented snores and late-night TV – no ghostly sights or sounds of woo-wooing from any spectral throat.

Disappointed but not surprised, I walked to the elevator. I would go down to the lobby and inspect the bar in the hope of sighting the spirit of Alex Johnson, who had constructed the historic building in the 1920s with all that era's charm.

The elevator came to rest on the ground floor, and the doors opened noiselessly. It was quiet and, dare I say, spooky in the main room, where dark beams crossed the roof in the German Tudor architectural style. The front desk stood empty, and I took in the long, dark wooden check-in desk fronting an antique cubby hole that could house room keys, then stepped over to Paddy O'Neill's Irish bar, appreciating the old-timey, tin type ceiling and the dark polished wood making up the bar. All was quiet. All was dark.

"Hello! May I help you?"

I jumped and turned, my hand flailing on the wall to balance myself. The night clerk stood before me, a smallish woman with dark hair and eyes.

"No... I mean I was just looking around, soaking up the ambience."

"Ah. Are you hoping for some ghostly sightings?" she asked. I could see a little smile playing on her lips.

"Yes," I said, flushing a little. "I work at a PR company for the state, and they're looking to capitalize on the haunted hotel angle." I was silent for a moment. "Have you seen anything? Any apparitions or perhaps felt any cold spots?"

She smiled a little. "Well..."

"Yes?" I asked, leaning forward in the hope of some unheard-of paranormal happenings.

"Well," she repeated, "I work night shifts, you see, and as I was walking past the bar." She pointed to Paddy's. "I saw something. I'm not sure what it was; it was more of a shadow, really." She shrugged as if to say, that's all I have.

"Hmm," I said. A vague shadow wasn't much to write about.

"The story is that Alex Johnson is keeping watch over his hotel," she said.

"I see," I replied, turning to give the charming Irish bar one more look. "Well, thanks for your time. I think it's time I get to bed."

"Sure," she said. "Are you checking out tomorrow?"

"Yes," I said, my voice rising in a question.

"Which direction are you headed?"

I hesitated, not sure what business it was of hers. "West."

Her eyes darkened as a look of concern crossed her features. "I was just watching the news and there's a winter weather advisory out for tomorrow, beginning about mid-morning."

I shrugged. "Thanks. I should be fine. I'm getting up early, so hopefully, I'll beat the snow."

She nodded. "Well, have a good night. If you need anything, I'll be here."

I smiled and watched her walk back to the desk, then I turned and made my way to the elevators. This was a bust, but it was a beautiful old hotel.

I stepped in, punched the number eight, and felt the elevator begin its ascent. The lights flickered as I stepped into the hallway, and I paused, looking up and down the corridor. Nothing. I walked down the hall, thinking about my next hotel stay the following day. It was a Victorian turned B&B out in the hills. It would be my last place to visit before I returned home to complete my article. I paused as I turned the handle to my room, thinking about the Lady in White. Whatever had happened to her, whether it be by suicide or some other means, hers was a tragic story.

I pushed the door open and felt a suction of air release as it moved past me. My breath caught in my throat, and I steadied myself, my hand against the door. *What in the world?* I thought. I shivered a little as I eased the door open, peering into the room and remembering that other hotel guests staying in the purportedly haunted room had complained of an open window that had been formerly closed. Normal, calm, quiet; my things strewn across the room, but that was nothing new. I was a notoriously sloppy packer and unpacker. My laptop lay open on the desk where I had left it, and I glanced at it as I stepped in and closed the door, locking it behind me.

I walked over to the window for one last look at the rolling hills before bed. Snow was falling over the city, covering the trees and roads with a dusting of lazy flakes. It was beautiful, like a swirling winter's dream. I turned from the window and stepped to the desk to shut down my computer and froze.

I had been researching the Alex Johnson before I had gone downstairs, but that was not what the monitor displayed. Instead, it was the site of my next stay – Hawthorne House, the bed and breakfast once a Victorian home.

I hadn't seen this particular picture of the house before, with icy snow covering the trees, allowing only occasional glimpses through the dormant branches. Their limbs pierced the sky like crooked black needles, sharp and dangerous. Deep shadows filled the snow banks, and how they came to be was anyone's guess, for no sunlight was apparent, only deep gray clouds, darkening to black on the horizon. The ominous feelings engendered by the landscape were insignificant though when one's gaze moved to the house.

Viewing the house piece by piece, with its arched windows and elaborate porch; it was beautiful, but the disparate elements did not come together to make a harmonious home. It squatted there in its hovel, the whiteness of the siding disappearing in the grayness of the photo. The small windows in the attic appeared to be hooded eyes, malevolent in the darkness of winter's twilight, and I shivered and wrapped my arms around myself. The pictures I had seen of Hawthorne House had been taken in the summer, when the overgrowth of trees had masked much of the home. I stepped closer to the monitor and studied the house closely. The entrance appeared to be a dark, wooden door. It's usually hard to go wrong with a door shape, but it seemed shorter and broader than most. There was depth to the opening, as if I could reach out with my finger, push through that door, and enter the house. I shivered again. I was letting the lateness of the night and the ambience of the Alex Johnson get to me – I, who always resided in the here and now. I reached out to the mouse to close the browser and paused. Perhaps it was a weak connection or a faulty signal, but snowflakes appeared to drift across the screen, twisting and spiraling as they swept around the house. I grabbed the mouse, and the screen settled – no movement, just a picture of an uneasy house, shivering in the cold. I closed the tab and went to bed, shrugging off my apprehension.

Chapter 2

I awoke shivering. I had turned the heat down before going to bed and was now regretting it. I stood up, wrapped the blanket around me, and shuffled to the wall thermostat. It read fifty-nine degrees. Good grief. I turned it to seventy and painstakingly made my way across the dark room, bumping into the chair as I reached the drapes. I grabbed the long plastic rod and opened the curtains.

Snow blanketed the city, but not the sparkling whiteness that dazzled the eyes, instead, the surroundings held the deep blue of twilight. The clouds hung swollen and gray, moving through the landscape, disgorging snow as they passed. I pulled the blanket to my chin, willing myself to warm up. I had contemplated going back to bed to allow the room to heat, but viewing the site before me, I knew I needed to get on the road if I wanted to reach Hawthorne House before the roads were impassable.

I hurried through my ablutions, shivering as I toweled off in the bathroom. I could hear the TV broadcasting the news, the top story being the weather.

"A big one is headed our way, folks. Get to where you need to be and stay there. It will be windy and cold today, but it should drop off tomorrow." I heard the other news anchor beginning to speak about the basketball tournaments for the surrounding high schools and mentally tuned it out, as I quickly gathered my things and zipped the suitcase shut. I scanned the room for any forgotten items and headed out.

The silent, sepulchral hallway from last night had vanished and was now a hive of activity. Guests struggled with suitcases, and maids moved from room to room, weaving their carts to avoid excited children. I flattened myself against the wall in irritation as two kids barreled down the hallway. *Where was their keeper?*

I crowded into the elevator that was at its capacity, and let conversations of the impending weather and discussions about whether to stay put float about me, as I concentrated on the decreasing floor numbers. I wasn't worried. I was driving a four-by-four and should make it in any weather. *I just need to get on the road,* I thought, irritated as we stopped at another floor just to tell them we were full.

Finally, we reached the lobby, the elevator slid open, and we burst forth onto the first floor. The fire burned in the fieldstone fireplace, and guests were busy grabbing coffee and speaking with the desk clerk who was ensconced behind his desk. He looked frazzled but pleasant in the face of the onslaught. I approached the coffee kiosk and pulled out my silver travel mug. I needed caffeine, and this was free. I made myself a drink and took a small sip of the scalding liquid. Thus fortified, I wrapped my red woolen scarf about me and stepped outside, glad to be free of the hotel's frenetic energy and the children's screams. Little slivers of ice rained down, stinging my cheeks, and I pulled my red scarf to cover my face. Plows were busy on the streets, and though I could see someone had cleared the sidewalks, snow had begun to drift in again. I stepped carefully onto the icy cement and walked to my truck, and was glad to see exhaust rising in the cold air. I had used the automatic start to hasten the warming process, but the vehicle was depressingly inches deep in snow. I left my suitcase on the sidewalk with my drink beside it and tried the door handle, but it didn't move. Upon further inspection, I discovered that ice encased the truck. I sighed. I would have to wait for it to warm, but in the meantime, I began brushing the snow, stretching my arms as far as they would go across the windshield and getting snow deep into my sleeves.

Irritated and now shivering, I tried the door handle again. Still frozen. I cast my mind around, thinking of a solution. A hot hair dryer would work, but there was nowhere to plug it in. Plus, I had never traveled with one. I looked at my suitcase that was quickly becoming a small snow boulder. My coffee! I stepped in my previous footprints in the snow and picked up the cup for a last drink, grateful that it was still hot. I walked carefully back to the driver's side, removed the lid, and slowly poured the hot liquid onto the handle. There was a series of crackles, and I yanked on the handle, which suddenly opened, almost landing me in the street.

I hurried over to my suitcase, shook off the snow, and turned to the driver's side. The snow was settling over the frozen streaks of the coffee, making it look like – I shivered again – like dried rusty blood.

Chapter 3

I pulled away from the curb, seeing no one else but a lonely snow plow, and felt my tires catch and spin as they broke free from the ice. I set my GPS for Hawthorne House and headed northwest out of the city.

My windshield wipers accompanied the local radio as I crawled along. The storm was moving slowly from the south, and I hoped it would give me enough time to reach my destination. I was reasonably confident I would make it, as I was treated to intermittent bouts of sunshine that turned snowflakes into glittering crystals, which were beautiful but blinding if you weren't wearing sunglasses. Finger drifts had started to appear on the road, but nothing my truck couldn't handle. My GPS warned me of a turn-off up ahead. I had been traveling the main highway without much trouble, but as I turned to go deeper into the woodlands, I felt my first stir of unease. Someone had plowed the road at one point, but it had filled in again with the increasing wind. I checked the GPS, which told me I still had a distance to go. I paused at the mouth of the evergreens, and considered my situation; if I turned back now, I would be heading right into the storm. Gone were the flashes of brilliant sunlight, as dusky twilight had come, turning the evergreens almost black, and I felt my first trickle of fear. I shouldn't have ventured out when I knew the storm was coming. I had lived in the Midwest long enough to know the dangers, but I was anxious to finish the story and return home.

I reluctantly put the truck in drive and began inching my way forward, feeling my confidence return as the trees protected me somewhat from the flurry of the wind, but as I traveled, the visibility worsened. The white confetti of snow made it difficult to focus on the road as I tried high and low beams to stop the dizzying effect. Ice had begun to build up on the windshield, causing the wipers to skid over the ridges, so I pulled over to where I felt was the approximate location of the road's side, put on my red mittens, and, gripping the ice scraper, opened my door.

The sucking wind caught my breath, and I gasped, feeling the cold peeling the back of my throat. I grabbed my scarf, pushing it around my face while stinging pellets of snow attacked my eyes and cheeks. I stumbled through the snow, thankful for my boots, and began futilely scraping the ice. I didn't have the strength to pry it away, so I tapped at it with the corner of the ice scraper, chipping away at the coating. Finally, having cleared enough to see, I returned to the truck's cab. I could hear the wind howling through the trees and started to feel a migraine coming on. I was in for it. I had discovered that when a blizzard was stewing, it followed a drop in barometric pressure, triggering a migraine, and I fumbled in my bag for one of my magic pills, hoping it would take care of it. I split it from the blister pack and let it dissolve slowly under my tongue. The weak peppermint medicine made me grimace, as I glanced at my phone: no reception. I wasn't surprised, but Hawthorne House should have decent service. I slowly moved down the road.

I rubbed my face, and squinted into the snow as I watched the trail disappearing and reappearing before my eyes. Surely, I should be approaching the house. I had been peering through my steering wheel at the rapidly decreasing view in my windshield, and would need to make another stop and clear off the ice or wind up in the ditch or the trees. I slowed to a stop and pulled on my mittens and hat, before grabbing the ice scraper and again opening the door and stepping out into the frenzied night. The snow was noticeably deeper, and I moved cautiously, securing my footing before taking the next step, as the snow formed little eddies about my feet like I was walking through an agitated stream. I chipped away the ice as well as I could and stepped to the front of the truck, intending to knock some of the ice off the headlights. I removed as much as possible, and feeling a trickle of moisture down my neck, reached up to adjust my scarf. I was disconcerted to see that the drifting snow had stopped momentarily, and I gazed about me, noticing the heavy burdens of snow on the evergreens, their boughs almost touching the ground. A sudden movement from the road caught my eye, and a pale shape moved just beyond the headlights' circle of light. My breath caught in my throat, and I could feel the blood pumping in my frozen ears, as the shape drifted closer to me, and I saw it split into another form. I stumbled back into the truck's headlights, losing my footing and falling into the snow. The wind whipped across me, and I could see the frozen particles of water shimmering like sand over the drifts. I tore my gaze from the shifting snow and looked back to the shapeless forms, my breath coming out in half a gasp and laugh. They were snow devils racing across the snow, bending and expanding, swirling and disappearing, only to reappear a short distance away. I stood up with the help of the truck's bumper.

I needed to get to the house. Soon, the road would be impassable, and I had no ability to signal anyone. I hoped someone would be waiting for me with a warm drink and a soft bed. I could not remember the name of the hotel caretaker, there had been too many hotels in too few nights. I righted myself and watched the devils pivot across the road, and then my attention was caught by a feeble gray light past the next copse of trees. It faded and shone again more brightly, as if pulsating in the night. As I watched, it flared briefly, insidiously, and then there was darkness, and I felt panic reach deep into my frozen lungs. I couldn't return; I would surely get stuck in the snow. That must be the house. It couldn't be more than a few miles now. I squelched my panic and climbed back into the truck.

Chapter 4

The road was fast disappearing, and it took several moments for the gusting wind to subside before I could creep forward. I felt the tires begin to spin and heard the snow creaking as they dug into the drifts. If I got stuck, I would be in danger. I inhaled the frosty air and glanced at the fuel gauge: a little less than half a tank. I had filled up before leaving the city, knowing there wouldn't be a sure opportunity to do so before arriving at Hawthorne House. The slow driving and extra stress from the snow had gone through more gas than I expected, but the house must be near.

I peered through the windshield, trying to focus past the shifting snowflakes. When clearing the headlights, I knew I had seen a faint light. The house had to be up ahead. I glanced down at the GPS. The destination flag was solidly in front of me on the little windy road on the screen, and I stepped on the gas and felt the back tires fishtail. My breath left my body, creating a small foggy cloud before me, as I raised my hand to the windshield and wiped the moisture, leaving streaky, moist contrails.

There! I thought. A shimmer of light shone through the evergreens, and I adjusted my steering, not taking my eyes off the gleam, watching as it grew stronger while I fought my way through the drifts. I started as the woman on the GPS spoke. "You have arrived at your destination,"

I studied the house as I picked the path of least resistance through the snow banks. The glow I noticed was a faint light coming from the transom above the front door. No wonder it seemed to appear and disappear, the leafless branches blocked the light.

I parked near the shrubs that lined what I surmised was the path leading to the front door. I could see snow reaching the top of the barren branches, ready to drown them in the ice. I stretched my arm to the backseat and gathered my laptop case and suitcase, tugging them over the front seat and then pulling on my mittens. This was not going to be pretty, and I hoped the caretaker was ready to take care of me, as I wouldn't be going anywhere for a while.

I pushed open the truck's door, and the wind took it, slamming it open and shoving it into me just as fast. I gasped at the ferocity of it and yanked up my scarf to cover my mouth and nose, as I forced the door open and wedged the suitcase between it and the truck. With my laptop bag looped around my neck, I eased out and pushed the suitcase free of the truck, not needing to worry about shutting the door as it crashed into the frame. I took a step and felt myself pitch forward as the snow reached my knees. I cast a quick, irritated look at the house. They were expecting me; surely someone was keeping watch. I took another large, sinking step. Evidently not. I threw my suitcase ahead of me and watched it slide toward the house. Then, with my laptop securely around my neck, I made my frozen way Frankenstein-like to the front porch.

My throat was raw from the clarity and coldness of the wind. Almost like ozone, so pure and white. I had underestimated the snow's depth and the distance to the house, though. What I had thought were hip-height bushes were, in fact, towering hedges, and I sank up to my chest; one foot lodged behind me and the other awkwardly kinked in front of me. I wrestled the laptop bag over my head, sat it on the crusted snow, and then watched the pleather valise slide down the drift, coming to lay beside a small evergreen. *Damn,* I thought as I turned to look at the house. I could see nothing through the swirling snow, just the fading glow from the porch light. Surely, they were expecting me!

"Hello!" I cried. "Is anyone there?"

The vault of snow poured down upon the landscape, making it difficult to breathe as I struggled to move. The snow seemed alive, its sole purpose to keep me stuck in the molasses of cold.

"Someone!" I screamed, looking in the direction of the house, wallowing in the pit I was in. I turned to look back at the truck, but even its relative safety was diminishing in the whipping snow. I pushed myself forward, trying to crawl out of the hole, rolling from side to side, the stress and rigor of climbing parching my throat. I felt sweat form on my forehead and then instantly freeze as the wind whipped around me.

"Help me!" I cried. I had been so foolish to do this when I knew there was a risk. One story about a haunted B&B was not worth my life.

I dipped my chin into the snow and felt the icy frozen water melt on my tongue. I was so thirsty. I could feel sweat trickle down my back underneath my coat. I reached a snow-encrusted mitten and tried to unbutton my coat to cool off, but my mittens slipped on the buttons, and in my frustration, I pulled them off and undid the first few, finally opening the coat. That was better, but the windy snow whistled through my sweater. Just for a few minutes, I thought. Then I would button up and try again for the house. I cast my eyes around me; snow had coated my eyelashes, and I reached up to brush off the encrusted ice. Where was the house? Surely, I hadn't gotten turned around, as I gazed around in bewilderment. It was all ice, all snow, nothing but the wind and the coldness around me in the dark. I gazed up at the sky and could see stars far above me betwixt the punches of wind. I was feeling warmer now. It was cozy here in my little hole. Maybe if I waited the storm out...

***

"Hello? Hello! Is someone there?" I heard a voice rippling across the drifts of snow. They sounded scared, but I was comfy in my snowy cocoon.

"Hello!" The voice sounded right by my ear, disturbing my peace, irritating me, and I huddled further into my secret cavern.

"Ow!" I cried. Someone had yanked my head back, and my frozen eyes creaked open to find a woman staring down at me, her mouth open, shock written on her face.

"You... taker?" I asked. My lips felt twice their normal size as I tried to make myself understood.

"Yes!" she said. "I'll take care of you, but you've got to help me get you up." My head lolled back as I looked up at her. She had a light scarf about her head and tucked into her coat. I couldn't make out any facial features, as she knelt on the snow next to where I lay frozen in my pit.

"Give me your arms," she said.

I weakly extended my arms, trying to grasp her, but my fingers were numb with cold, and I couldn't hold on.

"It's all right," she said. "I will pull you up. All I need you to do is push with your legs. Do you think you can do that? It's not as deep as you think. Ready?"

I nodded but was sure she couldn't see me through the thick buffets of snow between us. "Yes," I said weakly.

"Good. Ready... One, two, three, shove!"

I felt myself pop out of my cavern like a cork from a bottle, as I lay on the ground gasping for air, the pelting ice nicking my cheeks and eyes.

"Good," she repeated. "Now, I need you to stand up and put your arm around my shoulders." She was standing on the snowbank, and my confused mind couldn't understand how she could stand, as I had sunk up to my armpits. I rolled over obligingly with hands and knees on the snow, then I understood. The snow beneath my hands was now ice, enabling her to stand, and hopefully it would me as well. She reached down to take my arm, and I slowly rose, feeling my feet slip from under me.

"It's okay. I've got you," she said.

We staggered the remaining feet to the front stairs, the porch offering some protection from the wind, as the snow drifted down the stairs like a frozen waterfall. She walked up the stairs, holding my arm while I half-stumbled and half-crawled onto the porch. We paused while her hand fumbled on the door knob, as she pushed it open with force, and it hit the wall behind and bounced back to us. She gently pushed it open with her foot and led me through, and I felt the warm air hit my face like a sweet summer day and smelled food. I was starving.

"Let's get you out of these clothes and get you settled," she said, taking my gloves, unwinding my scarf, and divesting me of my coat. I was trembling with cold, and I could hear her tut-tutting, which, even in my half-frozen state, I found amusing. I had never actually heard anyone tut-tutting before. After removing my boots, she led me into what I assumed was the parlor. She pulled me to a chair next to a red flaming fire and grabbed a blanket from the sofa to tuck around me.

"I'll just be a minute. I'll get you some tea to warm you up," she said. "The electricity is out of course." She looked at me quizzically, as if wondering, *Wondering What?* I did not know and made no comment

Th-thank-you," I stuttered as my teeth chattered. "If-if it wouldn't be too much trouble, my computer bag and suitcase are-are out there as well."

She looked at me consideringly. "I'll see what I can do," she said and left the room.

Thank heavens, I was finally here. Safe and warm. I wouldn't tell my boss about this. Instead of thinking of me heroically, he would chew me out for risking my life. He was a nice guy, but he needed to get me off these soft stories.

I felt prickles in my toes as they began to warm, and I wiggled them in my socks, amazed the fabric was still dry, as I leaned back onto the chair's headrest and felt myself relax. The blanket was warm and soft, and the fire's heat felt wonderful. My eyes drooped.

Chapter 5

I could hear whispers deep in my subconscious brain, slithering and writhing about the neurons, peaking and subsiding until it reached a crescendo, and I realized the voices surrounded me.

"Is she awake?"

"Look how pretty she is!"

"How did she get here?"

On and on, the questions came swirling around me like the ice pellets outside. I felt so lethargic and warm in front of the fire with the blanket wrapped tightly about me. I struggled to dig my way back to consciousness, knowing others were watching me, staring at me. I opened my eyes, mere slits, and could see the fire still burning, the red-gold flames leaping up the black bricks of the fireplace. It crackled and spat as the heat touched my face and I drowsily looked around me, expectantly, wanting to match faces to the words I had heard.

I was alone in the room. I sat up with a grunt and grabbed the blanket to me as it began to fall from my shoulders. The chair I sat in was high-backed with wings to the side that did not allow me to peer behind. I rose slowly to my feet, feeling unsteady and disoriented, as I clutched the arm of the chair and I stepped around to view the rest of the room.

The wooden floors stretched before me, glowing and holographic from the firelight – ruched pale cream and vibrant patterns in the grain. I wondered what species it was: oak, mahogany? My warmed feet felt the coolness of the planks as I stepped from the chair and looked about me. The room was spacious, almost cavernous. The ceilings extended at least twelve feet if my judgment was any good, with wooden arches crossing the ceiling, reflecting the firelight and intersecting with each other, culminating in painted globes depicting pastoral scenes and ladies in long skirts and flowered hats. My gaze dropped to the walls. Wainscoting ran halfway up, topped with a shelf running around the room, supported by carved corbels. Other chairs and sofas were scattered about the room. A funny little chair had half an armrest and an attached table on which one of those old phones sat. Next to the chair, a curious cabinet stood with several drawers. The first row held a tiny and longer drawer, with the rows working themselves down the cabinet until the short drawer was the longest and the longest the short. Kind of inverted triangles next to each other. I stepped toward it and halted when I heard a door open behind me. It was the woman, the caretaker, who had pulled me from my shroud of snow.

"Oh, then," she said, "you're up and about already?"

I nodded. "Yes." My voice was croaky and raw, and I tried again. "Yes, I am." I said more strongly.

"I'm sure you're still a little unsteady on your feet. Why don't you sit back by the fire? I've some warm tea and sandwiches for you."

"Thanks so much," I said, feeling a warmth flood my eyes. "I mean, thanks for the food and thanks for-for saving me. I'd still be out there if you hadn't come out and pulled me out of the snow."

"Don't think anything about it. We all need a little help now and then, right? My name's Gabriel." She smiled at me, her teeth gleaming in the firelight. "And you are?" She was a short woman, a little thick around the middle, with short, brown hair and chaotic curls on her head. I frowned, wondering at my memory lapse of her name.

"It's nice to meet you," I said. Gabriel's definition of help had been a little bit more than that. I could have died out there, but all was well now. I was safe and warm in the house, though even through the walls I could hear the storm whining and churning. "My name is Rachael Wentworth and I guess you know why I'm here," I began. She looked at me quizzically over the top of her teacup.

"Well, yes. I suppose I do," she said.

"Right," I said. "I'm here to interview you and soak up the ambiance, so to speak."

"Yes, yes," she repeated, her head leaning to one side as if listening. I stopped for a moment as well. The wind was howling outside, reminding me of the rumble and shaking of a train bearing down on its tracks.

"When I left Rapid City, the forecast didn't say anything about the storm being this bad," I began. "If I'd known, I would've waited a few days."

"You're from the South Dakota area?" she asked.

I nodded. "From Sioux Falls."

"Well, then. You know how the weather can change." My cheeks were already warm from the fire, but I could feel the flush of blood. She was right. I had been foolhardy to attempt it, but I resented her criticism. I made a slight noise to acknowledge her but didn't comment. I had achieved my goal, at any rate. I'd almost frozen to death, but I was here. I could get her interviewed, absorb the house, and leave once the storm stopped and the snowplows cleared the roads.

"Have you heard how long the storm will last?" I asked, bringing the tea to my mouth. I had never cared for the beverage, but it was warm and sugared. I sipped it slowly, as I watched her finger trace a path around the rim of her porcelain cup. She appeared to be sizing up my question, deliberating on her answer.

She shook her head, the flames of the fire sending gold shimmers across her curls. "No, I have not."

"Do you have internet access here, I hope?"

"I'm sorry, but we do not," she said, her tone flat and final.

"Maybe if I can get my laptop or phone, I can get some signal." I looked around, willing my belongings to appear.

"I'm very sorry, Rachael. I was focused on getting you to safety. Your luggage is out there." Her eyes had gone frosty, and she waved her hand to the darkened windows. Her tone was harsh, critical almost, and I swallowed my impatience. Of course, I was thankful, but I would need to make notes by hand without my laptop.

"I can go out later and get them—" I began but stopped when she shook her head.

"I don't advise it. You were a distance from the house and it was only by sheer luck that I saw the lights from your vehicle. Whatever is buried out there will stay buried." I felt my hands clench and I willed them to relax. I would get them tomorrow. Even if it was snowing, it would be lighter, and surely bright enough to spot my truck and dig for my things. In the meantime, I would make do with pen and paper.

She bent to refill her teacup, her serrated shadow leaping up the dark carved paneling.

"You are here to interview me? About the house?" she asked.

I nodded. Of course, I was, but maybe this was her conversational process. "Yes," I replied. "As I mentioned in my email, I'm doing a set of interviews while visiting some of the most haunted hotels in South Dakota."

She was quiet for a moment, the storm filling in the silence. "I see. Will your family be worrying about you?"

"No." My voice cut across the room, harsher than I expected, so I modulated it. "My dad passed away when I was four, and my mom – she is currently out of the country."

"Oh?"

I nodded. It was none of her business. I didn't need to tell her my mom was working on her third husband, and that communication was sporadic at best – maybe a call at Christmas or on a birthday. We had lost our way when I was a teenager. As she wasn't the nurturing type, I had learned to be responsible for no one but myself. I quickly discovered if I needed school supplies or clothing, it was up to me to find the means to get them. The mass transit system became my friend, getting me where I needed to be, whether it be school, work, or shopping for personal items. I had gone to a small community college for my first few years, and my mom still lived in the area, so I took advantage of living at home and attending school. When she left, she sold the house, and I moved to the dorms funded by grants and student loans, which I was still paying on. I majored in computer science, intent on finding employment, and minored in English, my first love.

Life at the university was an eye-opener for me. I was surrounded by other students who were bankrolled by their parents. It was inconceivable to me to have that kind of support and not worry constantly about how much money I had in my checking account. These kids, and yes, they were kids to me, had just to text or call and money would appear in their accounts. Then, they would group like a large parasite and head out for a night at the bars. I had gone with them once and drank water with a lemon and artificial sweetener – a poor man's lemonade. That was my first and last time hanging out. I guarded my money fiercely, and they couldn't understand my refusal to order drinks and food.

"No brothers or sisters?" she asked. I came screeching back to the present, shutting down the frustration associated with those kinds of thoughts. *What did she care?*

"No, I don't," I said. My tea was cooling, and tiredness began to creep up my limbs. I wanted to go to bed and deal with all of this tomorrow. As if she could read my mind, she rose and set her teacup and saucer on the table, and then walked to the fireplace, her shoes tapping on the hardwood of the floors. She grasped the fireplace screen and moved it closer to the dying fire. Twining iron bars wrapped around the screen, enclosing a predatory bird that looked down upon the ground, spying on innocent prey. The tableau was almost oriental in its simplicity and fierceness. She stood for a moment, looking down at the glowing embers, then she turned to me. "I imagine you are exhausted, yes? Let's leave the interviewing until tomorrow and get you to your bedroom." She stepped to the side of the fireplace and lifted a lantern from a hook, then she pulled matches from the mantle, struck one on the stone, and lit the wick. After adjusting the flame, she stepped over to me and held out her hand, and I looked at it and then up at her. The moving light from the lantern snuck shadows over her face and cast dark pits under her cheekbones, as her eyes reflected the fire, the twin flames showing red in her brown eyes.

"I can manage, thanks," I said as I rose with the blanket still wrapped around my shoulders. Her hand fell back to her side, and she stepped away from me, the floorboards creaking slightly. I cast my eyes around my chair, used to picking up my computer, purse, and belongings, but nothing was there. I followed her from the room.

Chapter 6

The hallway was dark, cloistered, almost cave-like, as Gabriel walked before me holding the lantern, the light swinging to and fro, keeping time with her steps. Lighting my way and then leaving me in darkness as we traversed the wooden floorboards. My feet were noiseless in their socks, but hers, tap, tapped on the surface like a pick-ax tapping a rock. Framed portraits hung on the walls, the glistening oils from a century ago reflecting colors and shadows, eyes gleaming and smiles nonexistent.

Gabriel paused in our procession as I slowed down to gaze at the images. "Some of these," she pointed to the next painting down from me that was still cast in the shadows, "are of the original homesteaders."

I stepped beside her to view the portrait. It wasn't the textured oils of the other pictures, but instead a daguerreotype of a man looked back at me, one foot slightly ahead of the other, one hand resting on his lapel and the other holding a stick. I leaned closer to the wall. No, it wasn't a stick but a shotgun. He was stood before squat barrels with pans and tools scattered about.

I turned my head to Gabriel. The shrieking of the storm was growing louder and I could almost feel the buffets of wind hitting the sides of the structure. "Was he the original owner of the house?"

She looked intently at the man. His eyes were light compared to his face, and I wondered if they had been blue. "Yes." I felt a slither of air move up my legs and watched the lantern's flame flicker as Gabriel's face morphed into twisted shapes and then resolved into flesh again.

"Yes," she repeated. "His name was John Hawthorne and he built Hawthorne House in the 1870s. He came from the west and was obsessed with stories of gold."

I peered at the picture again. "What are those barrel-looking things?"

She grimaced. "They called that puddling. It was a practice developed in Australia where they constructed a large shallow bowl, poured water into it with the clay soil, and a horse would churn the sludge, letting the gold settle to the bottom. Hawthorne used half barrels and his—" she faltered, "his helpers would stir the sludge. When the dirt was suspended, they would withdraw the cork, and the muddy water would flow out." She pointed to one of the barrels where the cork was missing. A dark stream ran from the barrel as if it were bleeding, the dry ground eagerly sucking up the moisture. I shivered in the cool hall, and Gabriel noticed.

"Come, you need to get some rest. We'll light a fire in your room."

"Wait," I said, and she paused, bringing the lantern to her face.

"What is it?"

I pointed to the daguerreotype. "Who are these people?" She didn't look at the image but watched me, measuring me. "Those were his workers."

"But they look Chinese?" My tone made it a question.

"Yes, they also came in search of *gum shan*, the gold mountain." Her voice was flat and stony, as she turned away from the memories on the walls, her feet staccato on the floor in tempo with the storm's disharmonious wailing.

"Were John Hawthorne and the Chinese successful?" I spoke to her back as she moved down the hall. A staircase began to ascend along the right side of the corridor and rose to a landing where a dark window held out the battering snow. She moved up the stairs slowly, her hand aloft, carrying the flickering light. Faces and scenes appeared and disappeared as we climbed, the flickering shadows on the paintings bringing nightmarish images forth; disembodied faces and intertwining limbs, post-apocalyptic horrors, scenes from Beksiński. I turned my eyes to follow Gabriel's back. She still had not answered me.

She arrived on the landing and turned to make room for me, her head bent as if in thought, and I realized she was not ignoring me but fashioning an answer to my question.

"It depends on how you measure success," she answered. "Some are happy with a roof over their heads and food in their bellies, while others require adulation and power to feel success, and when those types of people do not get what they crave, all of those around them suffer."

I nodded, my neck crawling with little tendrils of cold that eddied about us. I could hear ice pellets hitting the windows, almost like sand being flung at the glass by an angry child losing its temper, and I turned to the sill and moved the curtain aside. Wave after wave of undulating snow flowed across the land, crashing up against the house to fall back and be picked up again in a vortex, as if it were searching for a way to breach the stronghold of the house; pulsating, probing, inching along the exterior. I shivered and stepped back, letting the curtain fall.

"Shall I show you to your room?" she asked. She held out her hand, the bony knuckles enlarged in the lantern's light, and the shadows they cast lengthening her fingers to disproportionate dimensions. I followed their direction and saw two hallways diverging from the landing, each darkened path disappearing to blackness where the lantern's light did not reach. I felt my throat close as unease spread through my limbs, like little teeth biting my stomach. I did not want to stay here. I did not want to be here. I cast one last look out the window. Frost had covered the edges, making an oval-looking aperture surrounded by icy lace where my weak reflection stared back at me. My eyes were shadows, and my lips a straight line of tension. I would get through the night and find my way out of here.

"Are you coming?" she asked, and I turned from the window and watched her move down the silent, dark hallway. She appeared a silent sentinel, leading me by lantern's light, the walls warping and distorting in the glow as we tread the floorboards.

Chapter 7

The room was vast, the ceilings stretching at least ten feet high, just like the rooms downstairs. Gabriel held the door open for me as I crossed the raised threshold. The storm outside was louder here, raging as it chased around the house, the curtains inhaling and exhaling at the windows.

"Why don't you lay down. I'll get the fire started and open the floor grates." She stepped to the wall and bent down, pushing the floor furnace open.

"It works as gravity heat and comes from the stove on the rock level," she said as she struggled with the vent.

"Do you mean the basement?" I asked, pulling the quilted blankets back on the bed. They had a musty smell, but I welcomed the thickness of the fabric. The bedroom air was frigid, and I adjusted the pillows and lay down. There was no point in undressing, as my pajamas were still buried in the snow.

She noticed as I slid under the covers. "We'll have to find you something to sleep in tomorrow. As for the basement... yes, I guess you could call it that. The Hawthorne family built their house on bedrock by chipping and blasting into the mountains." She had moved to the fireplace and kneeled to place wood and paper into the alcove. Then she stood, took a box of matches, and drew one out, striking it on the stone of the bricks. She bent and coaxed a flame from the papers where it flared and licked up the logs, causing small, brightly burning wood pieces to glow as the fire took hold. She settled back on her heels. "This should do for now. I'll check in during the rest of the night to make sure it doesn't die."

I had gotten sleepy watching her and the flames. My limbs had ceased shaking, and I could feel exhaustion creeping into my mind. Pictures of pelting snow, finger drifts, and the lone slightly ominous light I had seen of Hawthorne house from my truck filled my thoughts. My truck. Tomorrow, I would find my belongings, dig the truck out, and drive somewhere where my cell phone would work. My eyes slowly closed, mere slits, as Gabriel stepped across the room to stare down at me.

"I hope you'll be happy here, Rachael."

***

Tink, tink, tink. I dreamed of water dripping from a rusty old faucet... tink, tink, tink. It was annoying, and my dream self stepped across the floor, searching for the source of the sound, the chill from the stone making my bones ache. *Stone?* I should feel the cool floorboards beneath my feet. Still, the sound continued. I looked around me slowly, my body a few beats behind my thoughts. *Where am I?* I thought. *Where are the moldy blankets and the dying fire?* I stretched out a hand and quickly drew it back, my fingers wet and slimy. The wall was cold and rough, not the feel of smooth, cool plaster. *I am in a dream; there is nothing to fear here. I can wake up anytime I choose to.*

Still, the darkness stretched around me, suffocating me with its stygian blackness. I felt lightheaded and nauseous as a waft of sulfur slid by my face, dank and clammy. A brush of leather touched my hand, and I cried out, bringing my arms across my chest, protecting myself from the unseen things that moved about. I felt a sliver of webbing cross my face, sticking to my lips and then to my tongue, as I clawed the substance from my mouth, moving back from the cloying strands. A dull thunk echoed around me as my head made contact with a protrusion. I gasped and brought my hand up to my head, feeling warmth and wetness. I felt dizzy as I saw stars erupt about me. I needed to sit down and gather myself. *How can this be real?* I was sleeping in my bed. The woman, what was her name? Gabriel, that was it. She had saved me from my snow grave, and I was safely sleeping under a musty quilt. I spread my arms out; this... this was not real. I just needed to concentrate and I would awaken.

The sounds came louder now, frenetic and panicked. It was a jarring rasping I could feel under my feet. The thundering noise concussed my eardrums, and I brought my hands to cover my ears, crying out though I could not hear myself. Something was coming. It brought greed and terror. I could feel it slither up my frozen feet and settle in my clenched stomach. A thousand touches raced across my skin, little breathless squeaks fumbling about my hair and clothes. I frantically pushed at them, feeling even more take their place. Wet fur, leathery wings, and sharp claws enclosed me in a tomb. I was screaming, feeling a claw tear my lip, the warm blood dripping down my chin.

Wake up, wake up! It's all a dream! I screamed inside my head. I fell back against the stone as warm, pulsating bodies found hooks in my clothing and hair, chittering and grasping up my legs and over my bare feet, their musky, earthy smell ravaging my nostrils. I bent over, choking on ammonia, bile rising to my throat, feeling more landing on my back. Another resounding shock passed by, then as abruptly as they appeared, they left, screeching by me as I felt the wind of their passing.

My ears felt plugged by the sudden absence of sound, and I felt my chest heave as I struggled against my panic. As if tuning into a radio station, my ears slowly picked up my frantic breaths and flung them back on me as the echoes carried and bounced off my enclosure. I placed my hands over my mouth, trying to muffle the sound of my hysterical breathing, squeaking little sounds making their way through my clenched fingers as I struggled to control my terror.

A new sound, a reverberation, slowly encroached around me, and I struggled to breathe as the air tightened, refusing to enter my lungs. The sounds ebbed about me like snow surrounding an aged tree, relentless but still allowing the structure to stand. The air became filled with ammonia and human sweat. Dirty, dusty particles assaulted me, closing me off, claustrophobia ripping at my throat.

Then it was upon me, an avalanche of screeching and fracturing wood. The earth shifted under my feet, and I fell, shards of rock cutting into my knees as I crawled, trying to escape the dank, dirt-laden air. A new timbre cut the air; a tortured cry, a guttural groan that rose around me in a swelling crescendo, piercing my eardrums as I reached out to ward off the onslaught of anguish and hurt.

***

"Rachael! Rachael!" Gabriel held my hands, her voice panicked as she shook my outstretched arms. "Rachael, you're having a nightmare! Wake up!"

I sat up, gasping, rising from my stone tomb. I was in bed. I was here. I was safe. I pulled my hands from hers and brought them to my heart, the blood rushing through my body, adrenalin leaving me shaky and weak.

"You're okay," she said. "It was just a nightmare."

I gasped a little half-laugh. I had never had such a vivid dream, but here I was, safely ensconced in the moldy old bedroom. I felt my face flush. "I'm really sorry for waking you. I can't imagine—"

She raised her hand, stopping me. "It's all right. You're in a strange place and have had a frightening experience. Look..." She pointed out the window. "It's almost dawn. You stay in bed and try to sleep, and I'll get breakfast going and call you in a bit. Then we can work on the interview, yes?" She looked at me, and I could see the concern in her eyes. I am sure she hadn't planned on being snowbound with a crazy person.

I nodded. "Yes." My voice was crackly, and I cleared my throat. "Yes," I said again. "I'll be down in a while."

I watched as she walked to the window and looked out. "Still blowing. The drifts are almost up to the main window sills." She stepped over to the fireplace, and I watched her get the fire going, reds and burnished golds leaping up the chimney.

I lay back and closed my eyes. I was stuck here, at least for a few days. I listened as she stepped across the floor and then heard the squeak and gentle sound of the door making contact with the door-frame. The doorknob fell into place, its metal mastications sounding loud in the silence.

I tried to relax my limbs. I knew I wouldn't be going back to sleep – not after that nightmare. The wind howled around the house, spitting snow on the window panes, and I turned my head on the pillow to gaze out the window and felt a pain pass through my mouth. I raised my index finger to touch my bottom lip, and pulled it away to study it.

There was a bright red drop of blood on my finger, like a perfect red spinel, glistening in the firelight.

***

I grimaced as the hot tea came in contact with my injured lip, hissing between my teeth as I swallowed the liquid. Gabriel heard me from the sink and turned.

"What's wrong?" She stepped to the table where I sat and peered down at me, her brown eyes dark with concern. I had found her unsettling and chilly last night, but now warmth radiated from her, and I felt myself unbend a little.

"I'm not sure – I mean – I must have bumped my lip or bitten it, perhaps? When I was dreaming?" I shrugged my shoulders.

"Ah, yes, your dream," she said, as she placed eggs and buttered bread before me and sat down. She unfolded the linen square next to her and gave it a sharp snap before putting it on her lap. I felt my torn lip give a little quirk at her genteelness.

A sudden ferocious howl drew my attention to the curtained window as the storm encroached upon the house. Gabriel followed my gaze shaking her head.

"This one is certainly for the history books," she said. "I can remember terrible storms where we couldn't leave the house for days on end." I hoped this blizzard was not one of those times.

"So... do you think you bit your lip during your dream?" she asked.

I shrugged, unsure.

"Can you tell me what your dream was about?" she continued.

I set my fork on the plate, making a tink sound, and remembered what had first disturbed my sleep.

"There was a sound," I said slowly. "A clinking or tapping. It sounded like metal hitting something." I looked up from my half-eaten breakfast to find her eyes had lost their former warmth and were now calculating and testing.

"Yes?" she said.

Reluctance to talk about the terrifying experience flowed through me. What did it matter to her? She leaned across the table, waiting to absorb my words, and my eyes flickered away from hers. "I was in an enclosed space, I think. The air was dirty, like dust and-and other smells. Things were crawling on me, and there was an explosion... then I woke up." I finished in a rush, wanting to break the intensity of the atmosphere.

She leaned back, picking up her delicate tea cup, at ease now. "That must have been frightening for you." She appeared relaxed – almost pleased that I had experienced such a terrifying dream.

"Yes, it was." My tone was cold, infuriated at her prodding and then her apathetic attitude. *What a bitch.*

"Let's hope that will be the end of it. I want to make your stay as pleasant as possible for as long as you'll be here." She rose to take her dishes to the sink and began washing. I picked up my plate, cup, and fork and placed them in the sink beside her, then she handed me a towel, and I began to dry the dishes.

"I was thinking we could begin the interview after we're done here?"

"Yes, we might as well get started," she said as she drained the sink.

"Hopefully, the plows will be out soon, and I can get my things." *And get out of here*, I thought.

"Right. You'll have to use a pen and paper for now," she said. "It will take a bit longer, but we have plenty of time."

***

After we were done with the dishes, we settled in the parlor, as Gabriel referred to that dark, gracious room where I had first woken up.

Gabriel dithered about getting paper and pencils, stoking the fire, and bringing tea. She seemed nervous to me, as if unwilling to settle down and begin. Perhaps she did not want to indicate anything negative about the house and its history, or perhaps she was just nervous about her words appearing in print. I pushed back my irritation at her fiddling and strove to make my tone easy and measured.

"Shall we get started, then?" I asked.

I saw her shoulders flinch at my words, as if someone had raised a hand to her, and she turned from the fire, stepping to a chair opposite me to sit down. Even though it was morning, it felt like twilight; the curtains pulled, the intrusive snow advancing on the house, causing the fire to flare, as sudden gusts of wind crept down the chimney. If not for the fire, I would have had a difficult time seeing to write, as the electricity, of course, was still out. I was sitting at a small table in a straight-backed chair with the fire to my right side, warming my writing hand. The pencil she found for me was square-shaped with thick, bulky lead, and I couldn't imagine where she had found such a writing implement. I mentally sighed and brought the paper closer to me.

Of course, I had a list of introductory questions, but they were lost to me, buried in the snow. It didn't matter though, I could do this in my sleep.

"Okay then..." I began. "As you know, I am writing a series on the most haunted hotels in South Dakota. Your establishment," I paused and waved my hand around the room, "has some stories circulating about it, and that's why I'm here. To experience – first-hand hopefully

– any paranormal activity, and to record any experiences you or your guests have had."

Her nerves appeared to be settling as I went through my shtick, and by the time I had finished, she had a relaxed a look in her eye, almost pitying. I bristled at this. I knew it was a lame, soft assignment, but after this series, I would demand better assignments and harder news. Maybe – maybe I would look for a job at another company. I picked up the bulky pencil and stared at the paper, unwilling to meet her eyes. In my peripheral vision, I could see her picking up her teacup and taking a sip.

"Perhaps I should start at the beginning."

Chapter 8

A boy watched from behind Mission Dolores' adobe walls, as a small group of boys gathered in front of the mission, the setting sun turning their faces a livid red, sending golden rays up the adobe walls. The boy dug his filthy toes into the sandy soil and leaned forward to hear the talk between the boys and the great man who stood before them.

A light breeze passed over him, bringing smells of the ocean and old animal dung to his nostrils. His shirt hung from his shoulders, creating a great V-shape on his chest. The shirt was too big, and he had torn the long sleeves, leaving stray threads that tickled his hands. Irritated, he pushed them up, only to have them fall to his fingers moments later. He crept a little farther and stifled his panting breath, not wanting to be heard. The prickly rope that held up his pants was digging into his soft flesh, and he eased his fingers under the hemp to relieve the chafing.

The man stood like a beacon, the last light illuminating his flesh, while the boys were cast in shadow, dirty, dark things. For a moment, he was ashamed of them, thinking how they must appear to the man who stood in his clean clothes and washed hair. The boys were always hungry and never clean. The Christian Indians who lived at the mission would feed them from their meager shares and clothe them from castoffs. Every few months, they would entreat the boys to go to Dolores Creek and wash. They would cut Yucca plants with the boys and pry the soft ball from the roots. The boys would take the balls and jump in the creek, squelching them between their hands and making a great soapy froth. Sometimes, they would wash, and sometimes, to the Indians' dismay, they would throw them at each other. The sharp green spikes of the plant were harder to use but would create green bubbles, which they would rub on their heads and then laugh at each other.

The boy watched as the man bent down, opening a case next to his feet and he could see the childrens' heads bowing as if in reverence to the man. The boy leaned closer and then felt his heart pump with discovery as the man flicked a look his way, but no matter. He didn't signal to the boy or acknowledge him. He could hear the boys now, exclamations and whistles, and he wondered what would engender such adulation as he crept even closer. Then, as the sun dipped under the horizon, a bright flash of gold met his eyes.

"You there!" The boy stumbled back to hide behind the familiar walls. He could hear the other boys snickering, laughing at his reticence. Having been alone longer than the others, he had learned not to trust and be wary. Nothing was given or ever free.

He gasped as the man rounded the corner of the mission, and he turned to run, but the man had grasped the tails of his trailing shirt. He frantically squirmed, trying to rid himself of the coarse cloth, but the man had tightened the ends of the shirt and now held him aloft on his toes, brushing the dry pebbles.

"Slow down. Where do you think you're going?" The man's voice was breathless, struggling to keep the boy held. "I can't imagine you have a family waiting on you, eh, boy?"

The boy was silent but still struggled frantically, kicking out, trying to dislodge the man's hold. He felt his toes contact the man's boot, and the man laughed. "That'll hurt you more than me, boy. Now settle down!" He gave him a rough shake, and the boy fell limp.

"I just want to talk to you like I have your friends."

"They're not my friends!"

"Oh, so you can talk. Well, they're mighty interested in what I have to say, so I'm thinking you might be too."

"Let me go!" The other boys had rounded the corner and were staring, their mouths open as if singing. He felt little hysterical bubbles at the sight and in his desperation to escape.

"Listen, boy!" The man's voice was rough with impatience. "I'm looking for some help on a claim I have. I need boys such as yourselves to get into tight places. You're a little tall but as skinny as they come. How old are you, boy?"

One of the singing boys spoke. "He doesn't know, sir!"

"Hmmm..." the man said and shrugged. "Well, no concern, you'll do just fine."

***

The sun had set, and the dark blue sky held a thousand pinpricks of light, as he lay on his back with a wadded-up blanket under his head. The cool night shushed over him, laden with moisture, and he wondered if it might rain. If it did, he would go to the mission and ask the Indians for shelter for the night. Many of the boys would sleep in the dirt beside the mission, needing the camaraderie and the company of others as they slept. He felt no need. He was his own man, his parents a distant, helpless memory. He rubbed his face, feeling the divets of scars. He had escaped the sickness but often wondered if he might have been better off joining them in their simple wooden caskets.

No matter. He had something new to ponder tonight. The man. The man and his shiny lump of rock. Change had come to this dry, desiccated town; a whisper of excitement, a shiver of rich dreams. He had heard about the goldfields but had shrugged off the stories from the other boys. They had never seen gold, and if you had not seen such a thing, it was merely a wisp of fog; no sooner here than gone. But the man had a gold rock – a nugget, he had called it, and there were more in the fields just waiting to be plucked from the ground.

His name was Joshua Walker, and he offered the boys employment, food, and their share of the findings if they would accompany him to the fields and work his claim. The other boys couldn't contain their eagerness to join him, and though he was a distance away, he could still hear their excited chatter. *They were fools,* he thought, *easily duped and ready to believe in fairy tales.* However, one point in the man's – Mr. Walker's – favor was the strange pitted gold stone he held.

He punched the threadbare blanket, trying to adjust it to his skinny neck. Along with the boys' chatter, the pounding disturbed his slumbers as San Francisco metamorphosed. Even as night fell, eager men constructed a plank road stretching from downtown to the mission district, where saloons, cafes, and general stores seemingly appeared overnight to service the burgeoning population. The other boys rushed from building to building like starlings, chattering and frenetic, yet at the same time, he held back, observing and scrutinizing, wondering how these changes could affect him, whether it would hinder or benefit. *Perhaps Mr. Walker was the answer,* he thought. Surely, no harm would come to such a large group of boys; the man was well-dressed and clean. In his experience, the slovenlier a person is, the more likely they are to exploit the weak and vulnerable.

He adjusted the blanket again. He had no one to consult over such matters and had to live by his wits and instincts. Torn by indecision, he gazed at the night sky and tossed and turned until the sun crested the land.

***

"Good morning, boys!" Mr. Walker stood beaming, his hair burnished gold in the early morning light. The scene was chaotic, and the boy sidled up to the mission's adobe walls to observe. Little eddies of dirt rose from the earth as the horses stamped their hooves in front of wooden wagons. They felt the energy and excitement from the men and were eager to be on the move. The wagons' canvases breathed as adventurers packed them to overflowing, the men's shouts and calls providing a melodious counterpoint to the creaking of the wheels and the whinnying of the horses. Gone was the excitement and bravado of the excited group of boys from last night; instead, they huddled together like baby sparrows, afraid to leave the comfort and familiarity of the mission. The boy huffed at their lily-livered faces, remembering their laughter and derision from last night. He stepped farther from his perceived shelter as he noticed a particular group of people. The orphaned boys had noticed these individuals, and much had been discussed. They wore tunics and wide cone-shaped hats under which a single long braid hung down their backs. Their language was the cause of much hilarity among the boys, and they had all attempted to mimic the unusual speech patterns.

He jumped back as Mr. Walker's gaze roamed the setting, noticing the group of fledging boys and calling in their direction. "Come on, then! Let's get you boys up in the wagons. I see none of you have shoes. Well, we'll remedy that shortly."

His gaze fell on the tall, skinny boy by the mission, and he watched him scuffle across the dirt, his toes blowing up little dust clouds as he walked toward the silent group of boys. He could tell the boy was nervous and scared – all the boys were – he just needed to keep them calm and get them out of San Francisco. They would be less likely to bolt once they had placed some distance between the town and their destination. All the men were valuable, but he needed the boys to scout the narrow mine shafts, because it was much easier to lower a boy than a full-grown man.

"Ah, so you decided to join us, then."

"Y-yes, sir."

"What's your name, boy?"

"John Hawthorne, sir."

Chapter 9

I was mesmerized by Gabriel's storytelling. I could almost feel the grit of the sand and the boys' – John Hawthorne's – uncertainty and fear.

She had stopped speaking and picked up her tea. It must have been cold by now, but she didn't seem to care, her lips pursing as she sipped the beverage.

"So, John was a boy when he arrived in South Dakota?" I asked.

"Oh no, that was several years down the road," she said, appearing ill at ease, hands fidgeting with cup and saucer, eyes darting to the curtained windows.

I followed her eyes to the closed curtains. This was a drafty old house, and the material wavered accordion-like as the whispers of the blizzard winds picked their way around the wooden sills, penetrating the room's warmth. I shivered in the firelight. I felt uneasy myself without knowing why. I wanted to leave the house, yes. But why? There was nothing here but an older lady; the caretaker. I longed for the cessation of the storm, the freeing of my truck, and the ability to vacate.

Gabriel had noticed my shiver and she stepped to an etched trunk, opened it, retrieved a blanket, and handed it to me.

"Thank you," I said, accepting the covering.

She nodded, walked to the fire to add another log, and adjusted the fire screen, as the flames leaped up, beating the darkness back.

The blanket was smooth under my hands, the stitching almost microscopic; hues of greens, reds, and blues flowing together, surrounded by golden twisted vines. Dragons writhed on the surface, spouting ribbons of fire, and exotic birds took flight over cherry blossom trees. It was a thing of beauty.

"This is stunning," I said.

"Yes, it's been here since the house was built."

I looked again at the silky cover, amazed it had survived intact for over one hundred years.

"So, John arrived in South Dakota later, you said," I began. "What fields did he mine with Mr. Walker?"

She turned her face to the firelight, looking older suddenly, wrinkles fanning from her mouth to her cheeks, her eyes sunken, and little lines deepening to fissures on her forehead. Weariness etched her face, and I wondered if the stress of isolation and loneliness was hard for her.

"Do you have family in the area?" I asked.

Her neck crooked, snapping in my direction, and I sank back in my chair, feeling I had overstepped her boundaries. She chose to answer my first question.

"Walker and his group traveled to the Sierra Nevada foothills. Gold had been discovered near the construction of a mill; Sutter's Mill to be accurate. The workers had discovered a flake in the river, and the owner of the mill – John Sutter – wanted to keep this quiet until the structure was completed. As with any confidence however, three can keep a secret if two of them are dead."

I looked up from my notes, startled at the reference. Her face was remote, as if she viewed the past from within this frozen house. She turned to me; her eyes unsettled. "Can you imagine what it must have been like? The gold fields opening up, and hope in the hearts of these miners that riches were within their grasp? The impressions it would make on a young boy? The hunger, the fever of chasing those golden flakes. They numbered in the thousands, each intent upon staking a claim and returning home with gold-lined pockets."

A loud snap from the fireplace claimed our attention, a spark shooting past the screen to land on the glowing wood floors. She rose, took the little broom from beside the fire, and swept it back onto the hearth, where it glowed briefly before cooling and turning white and cold as if frosted over.

I stifled a yawn, and Gabriel noticed as she turned from the fire. "I think you still must be worn out from the events of last night." I shrugged. I was tired but didn't want to admit it. I wanted to get the background of the house and begin writing the story. I yawned again. I was stuck in this house; in this white limbo of frozen landscape.

"All right," I said a little ungraciously. I'll go over my notes, and we can pick up a bit later." She nodded. "I'll be upstairs if you need me," she said.

I watched her walk from the room. She was an odd lady, caring one moment and then rigid and impenetrable the next. I leaned my head back against the tufted chair, feeling my eyelids droop. Without the sound of Gabriel's voice and the scratching of my pencil, the sounds of the storm enveloped the room, the crouching lulls of wind pregnant with tension and then the unfurling shrieks hitting the house with snow and icy wind.

***

I came awake with a start and noticed the fire had died to glowing embers. My head felt plugged as if I had a cold, my hearing muffled. I realized what I could not hear was the storm's fury; all was silent, and all was calm. I rose from the chair and set the precious blanket down. My stockinged feet were noiseless on the floors, and I felt the slippery coolness through the material. Reaching the window, I pulled the curtains back, and found darkness, no stars shone, no wind blew water crystals. It was an abyss, a black hole sucking in all fragments of vision and sound. I felt my ears pop and a sudden tension in my back as if the darkened room held biological energy. A coldness began to form between my shoulder blades and spread to my back as if encased in a shroud. I exhaled, seeing the reflection of the weak embers blur as the vapor from my mouth rose to meet my eyes. My throat closed as icy prickles of terror crept up the back of my legs, and I suddenly remembered the walk down the hallway as the cold swirled around my feet and inched up my body.

"Gabriel," I whispered, my voice choking. She was upstairs. No one could hear me. *Was I dreaming again? Dear God in heaven, what was behind me?*

I slowly pivoted, feeling the muscles of my calves stretch with tension, as my hands fumbled for the window behind me. I felt the freezing cold of the pane, my fingers' warmth making them stick to the glass. No one was there.

From my vantage point, I could see into the hallway, where the staircase rose to the second floor. The wainscoting of the stairs appeared to undulate, moving in time with my quickened breath... in... out... in... out. I felt lightheaded as I moved across the room. I needed to find Gabriel. *Where the hell is she?* I thought. I passed into the hallway and saw the cessation of the movement, if indeed it had even happened. I stepped closer and saw the faint outline of a door with a chink taken out of the surface next to it. It was slightly ajar, providing a shadow that set it apart from the wood.

I watched in horrified fascination as my arm reached the entrance, my fingers crimping around the wood, pulling it open. Cold air rushed by me, blowing my hair back from my face. It smelled dank and moist, the sweet, revolting smell of decay. I felt my stomach wrench, and I gasped, the harsh intake of cold air hurting my throat as a hard, bony hand reached out and jerked me from the door.

"What are you doing?" Gabriel's voice was strident, angry.

I reeled against her anger and found myself back against the opposite wall. My arm hurt where she had grabbed me, and I felt sick with shock and the impact of the wall.

"I-I'm sorry," I gasped. "I'm not sure what was—"

Gabriel jumped to me and held her hand against my mouth. "Be quiet," she hissed in my ear. "Do not say a word. Do you understand me?"

I stared at her in disbelief. The woman had lost her mind. Lost her mind in the aloneness and solitude of the wilderness that surrounded her. Her hand pressed against my mouth harder, and I could feel the pressure of her bones hitting my teeth. I nodded and felt the moisture from my nose cooling on her finger. I needed to get away from her, away from this house. I needed to go home.

Chapter 10

Putting a finger to her mouth with her other hand, she pulled me from the wall, tightening her hand around my wrist, giving me no choice but to follow her, as she led me into the parlor. *Tis the prettiest little parlor that ever did you spy*, I thought hysterically.

I pulled back from her, and she stopped short, rounding on me, fury in her face. I quelled in the face of her anger as she seethed between her teeth. "You have no reason to open doors. You are a guest and will remain so."

Shock trilled me that she should speak to me so, and I felt a heady anger fill me up. "If you had seen what I saw, what I felt—"

Her face crumpled before me as if a muscle and tendon had given in to gravity, and her hands shook as she reached out to me.

"Don't touch me!" I said, stepping further back from her.

"I-I'm sorry, child. I didn't mean to hurt you. I didn't hurt you, did I?"

I stared at her, my face rigid, my eyes narrowed. "What the hell is the matter with you?"

She shook her head, and our attention shifted to the windows, where the blizzard's fury ululated and rattled the glass. We were in a maelstrom of ice and snow. Frozen. Abandoned.

"Will it ever stop?" My voice was high and uneven, bordering on hysteria. The stress of the storm, the house, and now Gabriel's behavior sent shocks of anxiety through my body.

She backed away from me and walked to a chair. Her footsteps careful and soft.

"I'm sorry, Rachael," she said. Her forehead creased, and her voice was low. "I'm sorry," she repeated, "please, sit down. I won't touch you or-or grab you. Please." With a trembling finger, she indicated the chair opposite hers and I walked to it, my feet dragging across the floor. I wanted to go upstairs to my room and lock myself in until help came. I wanted out.

I sat reluctantly and stared at the floor, unwilling to meet her eyes.

"Rachael, please look at me." I could hear sadness and remorse in her voice, and I let my gaze drift over the floor and up to her face.

"There, that's better," she said and attempted a smile. She needn't have tried; the effect was ghastly in the dim firelight, all bony angles and wrinkled skin. I averted my eyes.

"You, of course, can go anywhere in the house. I was caught off guard. You see it's been so long—"

She stopped speaking, and I broke in. "It's been so long since what? You've had visitors? Surely not that long. The tourist season ended probably a month ago, correct?" I said and then added with the smugness of youth, "Maybe caretaking is not the best employment for you. You must get lonely out here, and if you stay through the winter; I can't imagine not having anyone to talk with – to see." My voice died away as a smile of sympathy crept over her face. The hell with her. I was only trying to make her feel better, give her some advice.

"Maybe we should start again. You came here to investigate spirits or hauntings, yes?" Her eyes watched me intently, and I shivered at the intensity of her stare. I nodded my head, irritated. Of course, I did.

"Your hotels that you visit. People come; people go. Someone hears a rattle or knock in the night that they can't easily explain, and suddenly, the house or," she indicated the room around her, "the hotel is haunted." She paused and looked toward the darkened entrance to the room. "But I believe people are haunted, haunted by their desires, haunted by loss; caught in a never-ending coil where nothing else matters but their appetites." She paused momentarily as if considering her words and their effects on me. "They say Hawthorne House is haunted. It might be in the conventional sense, but it is not. It's just a beautiful old house built with good intentions, but now it is a tombstone."

Chapter 11

John would never forget his first sight of the gold fields. The panoramic view stretched before him, men and campsites as far as his eyes could see. He caught glimpses of the river where men sat by the banks, large flat bowls in their hands. As John watched, they would scoop up mud and sand, then observe the bowl carefully as they agitated it, allowing water and dirt to sluice over the sides.

"Boys!" It was Mr. Walker calling them from a few wagons ahead. The group of boys hurried to where he stood. They were excited to see such industry and wanted to take a pan from the wagons where they had seen them deposited before leaving San Francisco and try their hand at finding gold.

"We'll stay here for a few days and rest up," Mr. Walker said. "I and a few other men will be scouting the area. In the meantime, Freddy will be watching over you boys." He indicated the man next to him. John had noticed Freddy earlier and had come to find out he was a nephew of Mr. Walkers. He felt a thread of unease as he heard this. He and the other boys had made a point of staying out of Freddy's line of sight as they traveled. Freddy had made it clear to the boys that, as far as he was concerned, they were the bottom of the barrel and were to be treated as such when out of Mr. Walker's view. He shifted uneasily from foot to foot, the new shoes pinching. He would be careful to stay out of Freddy's grasp while Mr. Walker was away.

"All right, boys..." Freddy said, a mean little smile exposing rotted upper teeth. "Let's get the tents up."

The boys were familiar with the routine, as they had set the tents up on their journey to the gold fields, and they began unloading the canvas and poles in preparation. Freddy watched them, his narrowed eyes missing nothing.

A screaming howl rose over the camp, and John froze, his palms suddenly sweaty as he held the tent stakes. The screams rose to a shrieking pitch and then... abrupt silence. His frozen fingers cramped, and he dropped the rods, as he peered around the side of the brown canvas, his new Levi Strauss pants protecting his knees.

One of the boys, Samuel, lay in the dirt, as Freddy stood close by with a look of exultation and derision. Mr. Walker had come running and now was on his knees by the boy, his breath coming fast, his shirt fluttering.

"What the hell happened, Freddy?" Mr. Walker's voice cut across the clearing, and others turned their way.

"I don't know, sir," Freddy said. Mr. Walker looked at him from the ground, and Freddy's gaze slid away to find John's eyes peering from the tent. Freddy's eyes narrowed, resentment and malevolence covering his face as John witnessed Mr. Walker questioning him.

Mr. Walker turned back to the boy lying in the dirt. "Get me bandages, now!" Freddy flung one last hostile look at John and hurried away to obey.

Mr. Walker shifted on the ground, and John's breath squeezed, his line of sight unimpeded. Sam lay on the ground, a tent stake protruding from his eye.

***

John adjusted the blanket over his head. It was too hot to use on his body, and he hoped to block Samuel's moaning, who was lying two boys away from him. Mr. Walker had been suspicious of Freddy's part in Samuel's injury, but as there were no witnesses and Samuel refused to implicate Freddy, he continued to be in charge of the boys. John was terrified of such an accident happening to him and was vigilant not to draw attention to himself by staying out of Freddy's path. He felt comforted when he saw Mr. Walker's eyes on the boys.

Samuel moaned again. "Shut up, Sam!" one of the older boys hissed. Samuel began to cry, and John heard the thump of a hand impacting a body, as Samuel cried out. The boys froze, hearing stirrings in the tent next to them as Samuel continued to cry softly. At the same time, John's ears traced the sound of feet hitting the earth when a hand suddenly yanked at the canvas tent flap holding it up over his head. It was Freddy. He stood in the brown doorway, a lantern in his hand that cast macabre shadows on his face, making his teeth glisten and elongate, his nose dwarfing his small black eyes.

"What's goin on then?" he asked. His voice was rough with sleep and impatience. There was no answer from the boys. Even Samuel had strangled his sobs.

"I said, what's goin on?" Freddy hunched his shoulder and furtively glanced in the direction of the other tents. "You better tell me, or I'll come in there and make you all sorry, I will!" John watched from under his eyelids as Freddy dangled the lantern, peering at the boys' faces, as he stepped to Samuel and looked down at him. He nudged him with his foot, and John heard a groan.

Freddy knelt beside Samuel. "What's wrong, boy? Didn't I already teach you a lesson? Do you need the other one out, too? What good will you be to Mr. Walker then, huh? We'll leave you in the desert where the wild animals will make a right meal of you. Not much though you skinny runt."

Freddy stood and pulled his leg back, ready to kick Samuel, who was now openly weeping from his intact eye.

John felt something break inside him. The long days of loneliness without his parents, the hardships he had endured, the bullying, and the brutality of living as a beggar flooded over him, and he found himself attached to Freddy's back, pummeling him with his fists, scratching at his eyes, his legs tightly wound around him. Freddy screamed as John's fingernails raked his eye, and John felt the slimy wetness of the orb as he continued to hit him. All the boys had cleared the tent except for Samuel, who was lying prone on the dirt. The lantern had fallen during the attack, and flames now licked at the abandoned blankets on the ground. John heard the sounds of others, the men calling to each other, but the fury was so sound, so complete in his head, it burned through him even as the tent went up in flames.

He found himself roughly plucked from Freddy's back and thrown to the dirt, as Freddy screamed and held one hand to his streaming bloody eye. John watched as the men stomped out the fire, while Samuel stood with the other boys, his face slack with shock. All eyes were on him.

"What the hell happened, boys?" Mr. Walker said. He was angry as he walked over to the small group and came to stand before Freddy.

Freddy looked at him, his face wet with sweat and blood, and his voice trembled as he spoke to the man who towered over him.

"They was making noise sir," he began. "I went in to check on 'em and that one..." Here, he stopped and pointed a glistening finger at John. "He jumped on me back, he did. Started hittin and clawin. He made me drop the lantern, he did."

Mr. Walker walked over to John, who was still sitting on the ground from where he had been thrown. "Is this true, boy?"

John's voice caught in his throat. All were staring at him, and he could see their faces; some were eager to see more trouble, and others were tired and lined, wanting to return to sleep.

"Well, boy?"

"Sir, he came into the—"

"I said, is this true? Did you attack Freddy?" Mr. Walker's voice was hard.

"Y-yes, sir, I did."

Mr. Walker looked down on him for a long moment. "Git out of here. You're too tall anyway for what I have in mind."

"B-but, sir," John stuttered.

"I said, git. I don't want you here."

***

I flinched as Gabriel finished. "What a horrible experience," I said.

"We are all a product of our history," she said, "what we choose to do with it is up to us."

Gabriel refused to talk more about the house's history, pleading exhaustion, so we retired to our respective bedrooms after she had helped me light my fire. I lay on my bed, the flames casting shadows on the ceiling, and thought of John and the things he had seen, the experiences I had yet to learn about, and I shivered as I thought of the doorway under the stairs.

Chapter 12

I am in a cave. I feel the cool, wet, dusty stone under my feet. I stretch my arms from my sides and touch the damp, rocky walls, slick under my fingertips. Am I dreaming, or am I awake? I step forward and feel the indentation of pebbles on the soft soles of my feet. In complete darkness, I feel I am standing on the crumbling edge of a cliff, ready to plunge into an abyss. The cave breathes hot and cold air, cycling through the passageways. I feel it in my hair and on my face.

I am awake.

The cool, dank air slices through the fabric of my borrowed nightgown, and I shiver in the darkness. I feel the material brush my calves as the ominous respirations of the cavern breathe through its tunnels.

I lift my head and smell the sweet, cloying scent of decay. All around me is darkness. I lightly touch my eyelids to assure myself that my eyes are open. The darkness feels two-dimensional – flat; an x and y axis going everywhere but nowhere. My eyes strain to see some flash of light, a color, but there is nothing.

I step carefully to the side, feeling the grit under my feet, as I place both hands on the wall and search the surface. There is nothing but hard, sharp, slimy rock. *How did I get here? How do I get out?* I listen carefully and hear nothing but the incipient movement of the air.

The sound begins softly, a mere shimmer over the undulations of the air, scarcely louder than my breathing, as I inch along the cave floor, testing each step before committing myself to the path forward. I have no way of knowing if I am moving in the right direction. I want out. Therefore I must move – step by careful, tentative step. My feet make little scraping sounds as they explore the next few inches, and I pause in my efforts as the faint sound is now more discernable to my hearing. It feels as if my ears are stretching, needing to categorize the sound and dismiss it as unworthy of my interest or concern. Both hands are against the rock wall now, my toes and body touching the surface.

I listen, stilling my agitated breathing and dismissing the air sounds. There it is, a sound that rises above my respirations and the air currents, the slippery, slimy sound of consonants, the flatness of vowels. It whispers. I cease breathing to listen. Yes, it is louder now, and it is impossible to tell from which direction it comes. I edge along the border of the cave. Even in the coolness of the cave, I can feel sweat collecting at the base of my neck and trickling down my back. Slowly, carefully, quietly, I move. The whispers have increased in volume and tickle my ear, just below a voice, but I cannot distinguish words. Louder they come.

My steps move faster. I can now tell these sounds are carried on the winds of the tunnel from my right. They are harsh sounds. Guttural sounds. Terrible sounds. I begin to move frantically to my left, away from the source. Terror inching up my spine. I feel a soft brush on my fingers that touches the wall, and I cry out. The voices, if they are voices, rise in a cacophony, causing the walls to tremble under my shaking hands. The thunderous noise rises, and I start to run, my hands raised to catch me if I should fall. I feel wetness on my feet as sharp stones cut into them, but the horror of what lays behind me pursues me, and still, I run. My fingers splay to catch any ridges of stone that might impede my progress. Then it happens. My right foot comes down to meet the dirt, and I think the earth will rise up to greet it, but there is nothing. I feel my body slip away, falling as light as dandelion fluff on a breeze. Falling. The voices are harsh in my ear, reverberating around me. Little tendrils touching my legs, my arms, my face, trying to stop my fall into this abyss. Were they roots? Roots from nearby dormant trees? I reach out to grasp them, to stop my fall, and feel them willingly return my grip. I turn to feel their gentle touch on my shoulder and see not roots... but fingers.

***

I awoke screaming and Gabriel was by my bedside. I lurched away from her, my head hitting the plaster wall behind me.

"Please child." Her voice was ragged. "Please, it's just a dream. You've had another nightmare." Her hands reached out to me again, and I flinched, backing further away from her.

She noticed my rejection and stepped back. "You're all right, Rachael. There is nothing here. It's just us – you and me."

Words meant to reassure. Words intended to comfort me. But I felt nothing. I watched her pull a chair from the foot of the bed and drag it to where I sat huddled. I could feel the sweat drying on my back, making it itch like fury, making me want to scream with irritation, but I was unwilling to move. Unwilling to move my eyes from her progress. There was something wrong with her and wrong with this house.

"Can you tell me about your dream?" she asked. "Sometimes that helps." I bit back a shriek of hysteria. No amount of sharing was going to overcome these dreams. Dreams I had been subjected to since I entered this hotel. They were so vibrant, so horror-filled, I still felt the ache in my feet as I remembered my frightened running across the grit, across the slicing stones of the cave floor.

"I-it's nothing," I choked. "They're just dreams." I cast my eyes to the windows, uneasy twilight filling the room, as the storm continued to howl and batter the house. *Would it ever end?* I thought.

"Come now," she said. Her voice was no-nonsense, as if I was a recalcitrant child who wouldn't go to bed. "There must be something you can tell me."

I looked at her. Her eyes were deep pools in the dark light. I saw no concern or empathy, just emptiness.

"They're caves. I'm having dreams of being in caves."

She wasn't surprised at my words, and I wanted to scream at her – to shock her into feeling as I felt. My face felt warm as if I had a fever, and my feet and hands began to tingle as I felt the incipient signs of anxiety. It infuriated me that I was being subjected to such a stressful situation. I took my anger out on her.

"Why? Why do you want to know what I'm dreaming about? What does it matter to you? Why do you stay out here, when no one books during the off season? What is the matter with this place? You said it's haunted. So who's doing the haunting? You said this place is a tombstone, what the hell does that mean? Why don't you say something?"

My words had gathered force and volume as I spoke, and she appeared to wither as she faced the verbiage, flinching. I stopped, panting heavily, watching her as she sat in the chair. She looked empty of life, withered and desiccated like one of the dried brown leaves that blew over snow drifts, having missed their chance at hibernating under the snow. I felt remorse creep over me. Her life choices had led her here, and God only knew what kept her here under this mantle of icy isolation.

I moved forward in the bed, attempting to placate her with my nearness. "I'm sorry, Gabriel. That wasn't very kind of me," I said. Her wrinkled hands fluttered at my apology. When I first met her, I had placed her at fifty-odd years, and now I wondered if I had underestimated her age. She looked frail and breakable, as delicate as the snowflakes imprisoned on the frozen windows.

"It's all right, child. No need to apologize, I know staying here isn't easy under these circumstances. I am here for you, but—"

She stopped speaking, and I looked at her questioningly.

"I mean. I feel our time is running out – running out for our interview that is. Soon, the snow will stop, and rescue will come."

Yes, rescue would come, and I would be free of this frozen limbo. Free of this frozen house in the depths of these frozen mountains, but what of Gabriel? How could I, in good conscience, unbury my truck, retrieve my belongings from under the drifts, and watch Hawthorne House become smaller in my rearview mirror? There was something wrong here, wrong with the house? The land? Gabriel, the caretaker? Why did I care? She chose to be here.

The subject of my thoughts interrupted me. "Why don't we go downstairs. I'll make some tea and toast and I'll tell you more of John's story." She looked at me quizzically, a little more life in her eyes.

"Sure," I said. I was relieved that she looked to be recovering from my harsh words. "I'll be down in a moment." I watched her walk to the door; her steps were slow on the wooden boards as if each step aged her, and when she reached the door, she would cease to move, cease to live.

I sat in my bed for a few moments, my thoughts drifting from the uncomfortable scene that had just occurred to the storm outside and then to the caves in my nightmares. I glanced across the room to the fireplace; it was dying embers, white bits of ash showing in white relief on the floors. A bluster of wind rattled the window, and sounds of ice crystals hit the glass. I shuddered. I could barely see outside due to the effervescent frost creeping up the pane. Even if I could, the view was so austere I could not determine where the land ended and the horizon began. All was gray, all was black; melding in a smeared abstract painting.

I flung back the covers and froze, my empty stomach clenching, the bile rising in my mouth. Dirty red-brown stains marked the sheets where my feet had lain.

Chapter 13

I ran down the stairs, through the hallway, and into the kitchen, feeling the tenderness in my feet and wondering if I was leaving bloody footprints in my wake. I burst into the kitchen to find Gabriel sitting at the table, a lace napkin in her lap and her teacup in hand, balanced on her pinky and held with her finger and thumb. Her face was remote and white, so wrinkled I was reminded of paper mâché. My words died in my throat as I sat down. She returned to me then, her eyes slowly registering the kitchen and the person opposite.

"How are you, Rachael?"

"I-I'm fine, I think," I stuttered. "My feet – my feet are hurt." I raised one to rest on the opposite knee, and we both looked down, staring at the appendage, me in disbelief, her in mild interest, her eyes still full of shadows.

The soles of my foot were dusty but not bloody, not dirty. I hastily looked at the other one and found the same. My mind felt sick as I sat back in the chair. I knew what I had seen, what I had felt. I met her eyes and saw the same sickness. She knew. She knew what I said was true.

"What's going on Gabriel?" I asked. My vocal cords felt tight as I spoke. "What is wrong with this place? Why do you stay here?"

I could scarcely hear her voice over the dissonant sounds of the wind and the snow pummeling the house. I leaned over the table.

"Please, Rachael let me tell you more of John..."

***

John was forbidden to return to Mr. Walker's camp. The boys were sympathetic to him but didn't dare help him with food or blankets under Freddy's vigilant watch. He haunted the rocks and trees around the river, and at night, he would sneak into the campsites strewn up and down the river and steal food. He was run off several times, sometimes with words and sometimes not.

He spent many days watching Freddy. He would stealthily leap behind rocks and trees. He had been forced to give up his shoes when he was evicted from camp but allowed to keep his Levis, for which he was grateful. His feet became hard and tough, impervious to the small rocks and prickly plants. Some of the nettles became so embedded in them that they formed little lumps, and no scraping or pinching could remove the thorns.

Still, he watched Freddy and the boys. Freddy's eye had healed from John's attack but had a bluish cast that even he could see from a distance. He was like the blind people who came to the mission; their eyes so covered with integument they appeared white, and the boys would avoid them when they begged. Their groping hands and sightless eyes were terrifying to John. He couldn't imagine being in the dark, trusting each halting step would not lead to danger or death. He had practiced walking with his eyes closed, and after a few steps, he would feel the ground he was standing on become an empty abyss, ready to receive his falling body. His eyes would then jerk open, and he would see all that was familiar to him: the mission, the road, the people. The terrifying dark was gone; no black hole before him. He would shrug off his terror with a laugh but still watch the blind, fascinated by their calm acceptance of their dark lives.

He also watched poor Samuel. The boys were working along the river bank with pans of water in their hands. John knew they were panning for gold as it had been discussed thoroughly on the trail to the gold fields. The boys seemed to have little luck, but then no one appeared overly excited, perhaps to keep any gold found a secret to prevent thieves from stealing the precious metal and poaching on their claims. Samuel wore a blood-stained handkerchief for several days, and when he removed it, an empty orifice remained. The lid of the eye hung down, and every once in a while, he would place a smooth rock in the empty socket and tell everyone he had a new eye. It would eventually fall out.

The weeks turned into months, and the gold fields became a city of men and boys. Forty-niners they were called, every one filled with the fever for gold. They came from all walks of life, a poor father and son, to well-dressed gentlemen of the East, all looking for the elusive yellow nuggets. With the added population, more opportunities arose for John to become employed. He fetched tools and pans for miners, washed dishes, made food, and grew into his height. But still, he would return to the Walker group and watch Freddy. Freddy's ways had not changed, and time after time, John would spot him making things miserable for the boys and implementing unfair punishments; making them go without food and sleeping outside the tents where they were exposed to snakes and other wildlife. John watched. He had noticed Freddy would leave camp right before nightfall and return after the sun had set and twilight had begun. He began to wonder as the days slipped by. Freddy was not one to make friends, and John couldn't imagine any girl that would have him, even if there were girls to be had in the gold fields. He was curious.

One particular night, the men had quit early. It had begun to turn cold, and they had sought the shelters of campfires and tents. John saw Freddy begin his furtive shuffle to the outskirts of camp. He watched him step behind trees and bushes, casually looking back to the others to ensure no one saw. *Sneaky bastard*, John thought. He wondered if the other young boys noticed his snail paced exit. Perhaps. Especially Samuel. As John watched Freddy vanish from view, Samuel's one-eyed gaze lingered on Freddy's departure into the trees. Time to move.

John crept from his vantage point, fitting his feet to the rocks. Little pebbles made skittering sounds, but no one could hear from the talk and sounds of the camp as they relaxed by the fire. Mining the gold had been profitable for many when they first arrived. It had been a heady and frenetic time to be on the gold fields. Many had left rich, and others stayed on, hoping to continue to line their pockets. However, as much as they made, food and tools still needed to be purchased, and many were breaking even now or coming up short as the precious mineral became more scarce. The atmosphere had shifted from the heady early days to volatility and suspicion. Sites of potentially rich findings were fiercely guarded and protected with guns. John had noticed men from the West had been brought in at a cheaper rate and were now mining the fields. Their leaders kept a sharp eye on these newcomers with cone-shaped hats and long braids hanging down their backs. John found them interesting. They kept to themselves, speaking in a language he had heard back in San Francisco. They worked hard, often panning at the river when the others had long ceased. If he ever had the money for gold mining, he would hire the Chinamen.

There was no time to dream about that now as he saw a flicker of movement deeper in the bushes. He circled the camp, and his stomach growled as meat turned on the flames around Walker's campfire. The fat sizzled in the night air, making him light-headed with hunger. Coffee and liquor were being passed around, and he longed for a drink and surprisingly, the companionship of the others. His belly hardened with anger at Freddy. If he did not exist, John would take his fill of the meat and drink at the campfire. He shook his head, trying to dislodge these distracting thoughts. He needed his wits about him to discover what Freddy found so interesting in the dirty, dry landscape at night.

He had circled the camp and had come up on where Freddy disappeared into the night. He glanced back at the Walker camp and froze. Samuel was staring at him with his face reddened from the fire. His one round orb glistened in the firelight, his mouth an open circle, but just as quickly as he had seen him, he dropped his eye to the ground. John waited, sweat breaking out on his back and brow. If one of the men from Walker's camp found him sneaking around, well, he wouldn't think about that. He paused a moment more, waiting to see if Samuel would sound the alarm. He didn't. So John turned his back on the camp and entered the wooded area.

He moved quietly through the trees and bushes, his hardened feet finding pinpricks of thorns and dried grasses, but he did not falter. He could hear the wind whistle through the tree branches and the skittering of chipmunks as they ran over pebbles. He was used to these sounds as the wilderness had been his home over these long months. He had learned to be wary of the snake's rattle and watch for the telltale signs of bears. He felt at one with the wilderness as he moved through the deepening twilight. His hands touched the trees' rough bark, and he felt the sap sticky under his fingertips as pine needles cushioned his bare feet while he stalked Freddy. Freddy was easy to track as he expected no one to be following his furtive movements through the brush. A scattering of pebbles to his right caused Freddy to stop and duck, and John watched him in amusement. Freddy's too-close eyes and bleached hair peered across deep green branches, and he could hear Freddy panting as he scanned the area. John huffed again. A child could follow Freddy and he wondered why the boys had not taken notice of his behavior, and then he dismissed it the next moment. Fear. Fear of Freddy and his erratic behavior. Fear of being injured so grievously like Samuel. The silence reassured Freddy, and he began to move. John went with him.

They arrived at a rocky outcropping, the moonlight turning them white in the night. Freddy approached the stones, taking careful steps as he looked around the area. Whatever he had concealed, he wanted to protect. Silent as the night, John followed him, keeping a safe distance from Freddy and the rocks. He passed by a tree and then scanned the area. Freddy had disappeared. John hung back, using the trees as coverage. There was no way for Freddy to leave the space without being seen. John was sure of it as he noticed the rocks formed an enclosure of sorts. He then caught a glimmer of light where no light should be and exhaled. *Gotcha, Freddy,* he thought. He edged closer and saw an opening in the rock wall. A cave. He had reached the foot of the cliffs and began climbing the rocks. Freddy's shadow cast splintered dark rays on the cave walls; his breathing echoing in the enclosed space, sounding harsh and inhuman. A panting fiend. A merciless brute.

John felt anger swell up in his chest. Whatever Freddy was hiding, he knew that it boded no good for anyone but Freddy. He crept closer and could now see him kneeling on the cave floor. He was digging in the dirt and talking to himself. The whispers answered back as he piled the soil beside him.

"Think I'm good for nuth'in. Think I dunno what's goin on. They be sorry, they will. I'll be a rich man soon. Ain't no one to stop ol' Freddy. Them stupid boys, they be takin' the blame, not ol' Freddy."

John felt the anger spread from his chest to his arms and legs. Whatever malfeasance Freddy was up to, he planned to blame the boys. He thought of Samuel when he looked across the campfire and saw John. He didn't raise the alarm; his one eye had looked the other way.

John stepped closer, and the rocks betrayed him, as Freddy whipped around from where he knelt, almost falling backward losing his balance, his mouth hanging in surprise.

Cowardice and fear raced across his face and then were replaced with cunning and guile. *After all, John was just a boy. A boy Mr. Walker had banished from the group, a boy who begged for scraps and did women's work.* He could easily overcome him and leave him here in the rocks, never to be found. No one would question what had become of John. No one would care. He stood up, moving slowly so as not to cause John to run. He just needed to get close enough to get his hands on him, and it would be over – one dead boy amongst all the others who had lost their lives out here in this wilderness.

"No one would care," Freddy whispered.

"What's that Freddy?" John asked. "What do you get up to out here late at night?"

"None of your business, boy," Freddy said. He smiled in the lantern light, casting shadows from the corners of his mouth to his eyes as if his cheeks were cut and hanging.

John felt a slice of fear run through him, and Freddy took advantage of his weakness and stepped forward.

"Why don't we sit down, boy, and have us a chat," Freddy said. "Mebbe come to an agreement." He looked pleased at the word "agreement" as if he didn't have occasion to use three-syllable words often.

"Yes, an agreeeement," he said, stretching the word out and taking another step closer to John.

"What are you doing out here Freddy, and what are you planning to blame on the boys?" John demanded. He had taken steps backward to avoid Freddy but knew he would need to cast his gaze onto the rocks if Freddy continued to advance. Freddy would take advantage of his inattention and spring at him. John did not doubt this and knew that if Freddy got his hands on him, he would kill him.

"I'm just takin care of Freddy, is all," Freddy said. "Ain't no one else gunna do it. That'd be fer sure." Another step brought John into Freddy's reach, and John lunged sideways, falling heavily on his side. Freddy laughed and moved to grab him, and in that instant, John saw what Freddy was hiding.

The floor of the cave appeared to be burnished in gold, the dull glow mirroring the lantern's light and casting white reflections on the walls. Freddy was a thief. Miners and claim jumpers were shot for less than this.

"Y-you been stealing from Mr. Walker! You're going to be shot or-or hanged!" John said. His voice was breathless as the air had left his lungs when he fell.

"Who's going to tell um, eh, boy?" Freddy said. He looked down from where he stood, towering over the boy.

"I will," John said, moving to stand.

Freddy pulled back his leg to deliver a kick to John's head, and as he did so, John rolled onto his back and grabbed his foot, twisting it as Freddy let out a howl of pain, and fell on his back. John moved to stand, wincing as pain in his side moved up to his shoulder. He must have broken something. He moved past Freddy, who was holding his ankle and trying to crawl to him.

"Git back here, boy!" he yelled. "Stay away from my gold or I'll kill ya!"

"It's not your gold."

"It is!" Freddy lunged, grabbing John's leg and causing him to fall to his knees, as pain shot through him. He frantically reached out to his sides, trying to find something to protect himself with as he felt Freddy crawl up his body, pummeling him until he reached his head. His putrid breath crawled over John's face, and he gagged, his fingers reaching, trying to find a weapon.

"Whatcha got to say now, boy?" Freddy asked. The spittle fell from his mouth onto John's face, and he recoiled, stretching away from him. As he did so, his fingers found a rock. His sweating palm felt the smooth slipperiness of the surface, and his hand closed around it, bringing it up sharply. With every ounce of strength, he struck Freddy on the temple, and Freddy froze, all emotion leaving his face, his eyes blank in the lantern's light. He appeared to shake himself, and John struck him again and again until Freddy was no more.

***

My blood felt frozen as she ceased speaking. I could feel John's desperation and the horror of killing Freddy. I watched her as she sat silent, wrapped in a cocoon of warmth. The ice drops tapping at the windows gave me a feeling of tinnitus, incessant, never ending. Enough to drive one crazy.

"What happened to John after he killed Freddy?" I asked, wanting to redirect my thoughts.

"What happened to him, Gabriel?" I asked again. I felt I was pulling her back from the past, each decade passing before her eyes until they met mine.

"He took the gold, of course," she replied.

"How do you know all of this?" I asked.

"Account books he kept. Diaries from his wife. It's all here like frozen ghosts." She shuffled in her chair, stood, and laid the blanket down. "I'm going to make some more tea. I find it soothing. Would you like some?"

I didn't really. "Yes, that'd be nice." I watched her move about the kitchen, her steps halting and slow. "Would you like some help?"

"No," she said. "I find the ceremony of making the tea just as calming as drinking it."

So, John had stolen Freddy's ill-gotten gold. *What had happened then?* I mused. Presumably, John had traveled east to this area to build his home, and now I knew he also mined for gold.

Gabriel had settled at the table, her eyes focused on her dithering hands, as her fingers traced the lace edges of the napkin. Her bowed head seemed so fragile, so delicate, like a disappearing snowflake on your skin. She picked up the teapot, her hands as delicate as the bone china teacups, and poured us a cup. I wrapped my hands around the fragile cup, feeling it warm me, as I sipped the bitter beverage. Tea would never be my favorite, but I was becoming used to the acrid taste.

"Gabriel?" She raised her head inch by inch as if feeling every bit of her years.

"Yes, child," she said.

"Are you all right?" I asked. "Can I get you anything?"

"No, thank you." She appeared to rally. "I get lost in the past sometimes. It seems more real to me than—"

Her hands left her napkin and she raised them to indicate the house, then she looked out of the window at the heavy, gray snow, and I turned to follow her gaze and shivered. The dull glow from the windows barely lit the kitchen, and as I turned back, I realized her face had become more obscured, the darkling room despondent in the gloom.

I felt a shift in the air, an exhalation reminding me of the cave in my dreams, as a trickle of terror moved in my stomach.

"Gabriel," I said. My voice was a whispery hush. There was no movement or sound from across the table. She was now but a dark outline against the gray of the walls. My back tensed, and my breath quickened. I was alone here. Alone with this strange woman, snow tucking me in with nowhere to go.

"Gabriel!" I said again, my voice louder. I felt the movement of air again brushing my face, and I turned around, the back of my neck crawling. I moved to stand, and Gabriel's arm shot out across the table and, with surprising strength, encircled my wrist. Keeping me there, keeping me quiet.

"Don't move." Her voice was a thready breath, the barest of whispers. I paused as the air flowed over us. Inhalation... exhalation... inhalation...

Enough, I thought. I broke free from her clasp and stood, the chair toppling behind me. Gabriel rose as well, her darkened form a merest smear against the blackened gloom. Her voice hissed over the space. "Be quiet, you stupid girl!"

"What is going on, Gabriel?" My voice was shaking, but I was no longer whispering. She moved to my side, and I backed away from her and, turning, went to the hallway.

"Get back here, Rachael!" Her voice came demanding from the gloom of the kitchen.

"Tell me what's going on!" I said. My voice broke as another exhalation passed over me. "What is wrong with this house? Why do you stay here?"

There was silence. Complete silence. The wind did not howl; the house did not creak under the onslaught of the storm's fury. No grainy gray crystals hit the window panes. My ears stretched as they searched to interpret some form of noise, even the furious tones of Gabriel.

Then it broke over me. A wall of sound, a cacophony of voices and ear-shattering sounds of rocks thundering past me. I felt my feet leave the floor as I was pushed further and further down; I was screaming, my arms and legs trying to find purchase. I felt the presence of others; some were crying. Their desolate sounds brought pinpricks to my eyes. Fingers touched my arms and face, little hands, smelling of dirt and sweat. Their voices whispered in my ears.

"Isn't she pretty?"

"Can we keep her?"

Chapter 14

I lay on the floor, with Gabriel's arms cradling my head, her brown eyes now warm with concern. The noise was gone, the air was still, and the only sound was the ever-present storm encroaching on the house.

"Are you all right?" Gabriel asked. I stared at her and then sat up, shaking off her arms, as I glanced around the room and my eyes found their way out into the hallway to the door under the stairs.

"Where does that go?" I asked. She was silent.

"Is it just a little cubbyhole – for storage or something?" I persisted. She was still mute. I stood up and felt myself sway for a moment, placing my hand on the plaster walls to steady myself, and I looked at Gabriel, who remained on the floor. Her hands had fallen empty, the delicate bones almost skeletal.

"Gabriel?"

She looked up at me then, and I saw pity and hopelessness in her eyes.

"It'll be okay, Gabriel. We'll be rescued soon, and we—" I paused. I didn't know if she wanted to leave here, but I sure as hell did. "We..." I said firmly. "We can leave this place. There are other jobs you can find. I'll help you," I promised, then wondered where that came from. I took care of myself and no one else. Certainly not some aging woman with no family. Then, it occurred to me that I really had no family as well. Would I be just like Gabriel as I got older? Alone in some godforsaken house, with no one to talk to or care about... and no one to care about me?

She turned to look at the door, and I followed her gaze and felt nauseous with anxiety, remembering the pulsating rhythm.

"That is the door to John's goldmine."

***

I helped Gabriel from the floor, and we staggered into the parlor, where I built a fire under her guidance and wrapped her in the beautiful silken blanket. Her face had been ashen in the hallway, but now the fire gave it a false ruddy glow. She seemed to have shrunk since I met her, closing in on herself like the snow was closing in on the house, encasing us in a frozen tomb. I felt the coolness from the leaky windows brush my arms and I shivered. Gabriel had said this house was a tombstone.

I moved my chair closer to the fire, wincing as it scraped against the wooden floors. The sound caught her attention, and her eyes showed signs of life, signs of being present.

"Are you okay, Gabriel?" She nodded, an old woman nod, slow and careful; the firelight elongating and then compressing her wrinkles.

"What is going on in this house?" I asked. "Why do I have these dreams of caves? I feel the presence of others. I know you feel these things too. I also feel danger. I need to know what is happening here! What is happening to me!" My voice rose as I spoke. I hated to lose control, but these events were terrifying. I wanted to – I gulped –

survive seemed melodramatic, but that was how I felt. I needed to leave this house whole, with mind and body intact.

"Yes," she replied and was silent. I wanted to stand up and shake her bony shoulders until they snapped under my fingers.

"Yes, what!" I said, impatience filling my body. "What do you know? What do you see?"

"I feel it all, Rachael. Every shiver, every whisper, every sound... but I am old now. My will is weak. *I* am weak.

"You need to leave this place! It's driving you crazy. No one would stay here and willingly be subjected to these-these things!" I said. My voice was firm, trying to cajole her into leaving when rescue came.

"This is my home," she said. "I won't be leaving."

"Gabriel, it's your *job*!" I said. "You don't need to stay here."

"I do, and in time, you will understand," she said, holding out her hands to the fire's warmth. There was such fragility in those small hands you could almost perceive the light passing through as she held them to the blaze.

***

John stood on the wharf, his back braced on the pilings as he waited for the ships to disgorge their human and cargo goods. The sun found its way through the small holes of his wicker hat, and he felt sweat gather on his brow and slip down his face. The seagulls fluttered overhead, screaming and screeching as they dove at fish entrails and foodstuffs. He kicked at one as it came too close to him and his lunch of boiled eggs and potatoes. He had been waiting since dawn for a particular ship to dock. It had sailed from a southern region of China called

Taishan with what he hoped were able-bodied Chinamen. The ship had spent days in the busy harbor waiting to unload.

Bells clanged above him, and he pushed away from the piling and rested his hand on the wood, feeling the dry splinters flake under his thumb as he worried the dried piling. The water lapped at the wharf, sending spray up the rocks and onto the docks, and he licked his lips, tasting the water's saltiness as he watched the seagulls flutter, looking for insects in the clinging seaweed hanging on the rocks.

The *Clear Mountain* ship was due to dock today, and he felt his heart race in his chest. This was the last step after months of planning and the last few years of work. He had hoarded his twice stolen gold, and the amount had grown through an investment in a saloon. He had pulled his money from the saloon yesterday. The owner was not pleased, and they had almost come to blows, but John had prevailed and left with his hoard and a case of whiskey. The owner had spat on him as he picked up the case, but John had resumed walking, letting the saloon doors crash against the walls in his fury at the man.

He jumped aside as porters rushed by him, ready to unload *Clear Mountain*. It was a difficult task as the porters needed to wade across half a mile of muddy tidal flats to the ships and haul supplies and people back to the shoreline. Lilting, swaying ships filled the harbor, caught in the muddy water, unable to move, their riggings down to prevent entanglement with the other vessels. Some of the more decrepit ships were knowingly abandoned by their owners and left to rot. At the same time, entrepreneurs purchased ships closer to the shoreline and built them up with dirt and stone to become businesses, where one could walk the plank and enter a saloon or brothel.

As San Francisco welcomed thousands of gold seekers, land became a precious commodity, and the San Franciscan politicians had devised a solution. They offered the purchase of water lots if owners placed pilings and fencing around the property. This practice gave way to hulk undertakers, who, in the dead of night, would float their vessels to these valuable properties and sink them, claiming the land as part of their salvage.

"Ahoy there!" a porter called to the men on the docks who stood smoking and spitting into the muddy water. The motley group of men looked down at what followed the porter. A snake of humanity, like a Chinese celebration of Chinamen, women, and children, all miserable, all muddy slogged in the mud behind him, their faces fearful.

"Are these ours then?" one of the men called down. "Bring 'em up and let's look at 'em." He spat near the porter's feet, and a seagull swooped down in furtive movements to investigate. The porter looked up at the man angrily, his eyes squinting in the sun. Mud crisscrossed his face, settling into the lines about his eyes and mouth, and his clothes were little better.

"Damn you then," he said, turning to the line of people behind him. "All right, git up there, then." He addressed the men assembled on the wharf. "Capt'n comin to dole out this boodle."

One of the men guffawed. "I say we take what we like and get 'em to work."

"Nah you won't!" the porter said. "The Capt'n will be comin!" He looked around, hoping to see the man. The wrinkles in his face relaxed as he spotted men rowing the captain to shore, and he raised his hand and cupped his mouth. "Ahoy there Capt'n. Here we be!"

The captain looked languidly over to where the porter and the group of Chinese were standing, and he raised a hand to acknowledge him and directed the rowers, who dipped the oars in the muddy water, turning the boat toward the group on the wharf. Bits of mud splashed up, and John could see the captain wiping his face in irritation, the movements of his mouth sharp as he chastised the rowmen, and their arm movements slowed as they more carefully navigated the boat.

They had reached a standstill, where the mud didn't allow for further movement, and the captain stood, motioning to the men to bring his belongings. They entered the tidal flats and, squelching, moved past the long line of Chinese.

The porters lifted the captain and his belongings onto the wharf, where the men immediately surrounded him, all vying for his attention and their pick of Chinese workers.

"Quiet then!" he roared. "I have me list of who has been contracted. So, all of you, pipe down!" He turned to his chest, opened it, and retrieved a sheaf of papers. Then he looked through the lists and began to call out Chinese names and the men they had been contracted to. John stood among them, waiting for his workers.

"Here there, then back up." One of the men elbowed John out of the way. "You wait your turn. We've been at this much longer than you," he continued, his lip curling so John could see his brown and pitted teeth. Bits of tobacco stuck to his lips, and dried bits clung to his beard – the man stank.

John felt anger simmer in his gut. He had paid for these workers and did not want the weak-looking ones or those who also brought their families.

"Watch yourself," John said. "I've bought and paid for these men. I have the documents to prove it."

"I don't care what you have," the man said. "You'll wait until I say."

The captain stood a few yards away, oblivious to their argument, as the men took the Chinese away to their new way of life.

John pushed past the man, intent on getting the captain's attention; he'd be damned if his plans would be thwarted at this late stage. But, the brute sidestepped, blocking John's path, his mouth curved in a smile, hoping to get a rise from him. However, John shouldered him out of the way, wanting to avoid the fight the man was spoiling for.

Suddenly, the force of the man's fist on the side of his head brought John to his knees. He could hear the others laughing as he shook his head, his ears ringing as the man walked by him. John launched himself at the man's knees, toppling him so he lay flat on the wharf's desiccated boards, then John rolled onto his back. His hat had come off, and he gazed blearily up at the sky, little pinpricks of light blocking his vision. He heard the other man roar and felt the pounding of the floorboards as he ran at John, sitting atop his chest and beating him until the sun and the sky were no more.

***

He awoke later as brilliant reds and golds streaked the sky. He moved his head and groaned as nausea overtook him, and he blearily opened his eyes. The twinkling stars were real now as the sun set. Blood had dried on his face, and he could taste its tang as he tried to spit but could not form enough moisture to do so. He rolled over on his side, a deep groan erupting from him. He could see the sluggish, muddy water lapping the shoreline between the wooden slats of the wharf. Insects moved across the surface, buoyed by the tension of the thick sludge. The "caw caw" of the seagulls pounded at his head, and he wished for a gun as he pushed himself to his knees and grimaced. His whole body was sore and battered. He wiped his mouth as his lips began to bleed again and noted his split knuckles. *Hopefully, that means I landed a few blows of my own,* he thought.

He became aware of other sounds, movements, and whispers; sounds of gurgling and a hushed cry, as he turned sharply and felt his brain slosh as it righted itself. A group of people stood before him: a few men, women, and several children. These would be his miners.

John rolled over onto his back and gazed up at the stars. All of his plans, all of his work and dreams had gone up in smoke. The bastards had left him with the dregs of the Chinese. He cast a bleary eye in their direction, and they all stared back. He could see fear and uncertainty from the men and women, while the little ones stood behind what he assumed were their mothers, their almond eyes rounded with apprehension. He sighed and gazed back to the heavens, considering his options. He could hunt down the captain of the ship and demand better workers, or find the man who had hit him and take his workers by force.

Both choices were fraught with failure though. He would have difficulty locating the man who had left him unconscious on the wharf. If the man had any sense, he would be long gone on his way to the gold mines. John assumed the captain could not provide him with other workers; the other men had picked over the best, leaving the worst for him. *Damn it all to hell.* He knew the gold fields of the Sierras were drying up and he had heard murmurs of gold farther east in the Dakota Territory. He did not have time to conscript more workers and wait for the three-month passage by water. Who was to say it wouldn't happen again? But next time, he would not be taken advantage of. He would be ready with a gun and remove any threat standing between him and his dreams of gold. *That rat bastard.*

He rolled to his knees and felt his head swim. Leaning over, he spat what little moisture he had onto the wood, blood and mucous dripping down to the muddy water below.

"Any one of you speak English?" he asked, swaying as he rose. The moonlight shone on the children's heads, making white streaks in their black hair. The older Chinese regarded him, their eyes glinting from under their conical-shaped hats. No one spoke.

John heard the sound of revelry and drunken noises from the bars that lined the bay. He glanced their way – fools, wasting good money and time on drunkenness and habits that led nowhere and achieved nothing. He looked back at the motley group assembled on the wharf. He hoped they knew what laid in store for them. He would give no quarter in the search for his dreams.

"Come!" he barked at them and gesticulated with his hand. They stood there unmoving.

"I said, come! You belong to me!"

A man stepped away from the group, bowing his head, and then looked at John. "We come, sir. My name, Bao."

"Oh, so you can speak English. Well, now you're the foreman, and your first task is to keep all these," he waved his arm to encompass the group, "your compadres, in line. Understand?"

Bao was silent, trying to follow John's complicated sentence. John saw this and lashed out in frustration. His head hurt, he had been humiliated, and he had lost time. He had hoped to have his miners on the train to Omaha today.

He pointed his finger at Bao and then at the huddled group. "You," he told Bao, "watch," he flung his arm at the others, and he watched in satisfaction as they flinched from his anger.

"Shi de," said Bao, nodding his head.

"No Chinese talk!" John said. "English only!"

"Yes," said Bao. "No Chinese." He turned to pull a woman and child forward. "Wife, Jin, child Bi—"

John cut him off. "I don't care. You've wasted enough of my time today." He stalked down the creaking planks, his boots thumping them, punishing them as he walked.

Bao looked back toward the others and motioned with his arm. "Come."

Even though the wharf was sturdy under their feet, the shifting moonlight dazzled the eyes, teasing the newly landed group as they traversed the wood, their legs unsteady.

John was furious about the children. He could put the women to work, but the younglings were more mouths to feed with little benefit to him. Perhaps he should take a wife. She would be responsible for the children when the adults mined. Maybe she would bear him a son, and he would teach him how to mine gold and protect what was his. No son of his would be left on the street to fend for himself. He grunted in satisfaction. He had a plan.

***

John led his group into the streets of San Francisco. He had planned to rent a room in one of the boarding houses for the men, but with the addition of the women and children, he felt sure no boarding house would allow him to rent only one room for all. No matter, they would sleep under the stars. San Francisco was a tent city. The surrounding landscape was alive with glowing canvas shelters like Chinese lanterns. *They should feel right at home,* he thought. He tossed a glance over his shoulder and noted with satisfaction that Bao kept the others together while carrying two children. He felt another sting of irritation at the situation the man on the wharf had thrust upon him. If he ever again laid eyes upon him...

He led them down to a field where others camped awaiting the train. It was relatively empty as people had vacated the area earlier that day to head east. The train he should have been on. He pushed the pointless thoughts aside.

"Bao!" He motioned with his arm, and Bao set the children down and hurried over to him.

"Sleep here." John pointed to the area around him. His trunks and supplies were on the train that left today, and he needed to speak with the trainmaster for assurance they would be waiting when he arrived.

Bao looked about him. There was nothing but hard-packed earth. No shelter. No water. The air was cool as it blew in from the ocean and promised to be colder as the night progressed. He looked back at his countrymen and his family. He could see his young daughter shivering even though Jin held her tightly.

He turned back to John. "Warm," he said and then wrapped his arms about himself.

"I know," John said, striving to keep his temper in check. "You," he pointed at Bao, "come." And then he pointed at the rest. "Stay."

Bao turned to the group and held up his hand, indicating to them to stay, and he turned back to John. "Yes."

John nodded and began to walk toward Fourth and Brannan Street, the location of the one-story train depot. He and Bao walked up the wooden stairs to the platform where passengers and freight were loaded and unloaded. He stepped across the planks, avoiding others who loitered there to consult the timetable posted on the outside wall. A connecting train was leaving tomorrow afternoon, and if he read the schedules correctly, they would make it to Omaha in four days. He had lost the money on the tickets meant for today, but hopefully, no more time would be wasted.

He sighed and turned to Bao. "Food and blankets." Bao nodded, and they left the platform.

***

It was late when they returned. Someone had built a fire, and his workers sat huddled around the embers in varying states of consciousness. All of the children were sleeping, along with several of the women. The men stood when John and Bao arrived with supplies, and they began to distribute the coarse blankets, beans, and dried meat. The women woke the children to take a few bites, but they were soon sleeping, some still with mouths full of beans, which the women had to remove to prevent them from choking.

John sat on the sandy soil and removed his boots. His feet were wet from sweat from the day, and he needed to take off his socks and let them dry out before morning. He situated them on a nearby rock and dug his toes in the dirt, which transported him back to years ago when he was a boy peering around the mission at Mr. Walker. He had committed untasteful acts to get to where he was today but did not regret any of them and would do them again if the situation was warranted.

He looked about their impromptu camp. The children were the weak link in his plans. He could force the adults to leave them behind; let them fend for themselves on the streets like he had done. He had made it after all. But as he watched Bao and his attentiveness to his wife and child – what were their names? – he could not remember; he feared he would have difficulty forcing them to leave their progeny. He knew the men would also stay if he left the women and children.

It was important they get out of San Francisco as soon as possible. He knew Chinamen used to receive wages of twenty dollars a day to lay rail lines – a fortune to the them – and he didn't want them to abandon him for easier, more lucrative prospects. Even the Chinese launders made more money than the prospectors now by carefully washing the miners' clothing and letting flakes settle to the bottom of the wash tubs.

He stretched out on the ground and placed a rolled blanket under his head. Morning would come soon, and he must be on that train. He had hidden much of his gold in his trunks and chests, being wary of banks. He had a pocket sewn into the lining of his jacket, where he had stashed paper bills. He felt fortunate that the man who had laid him flat had not found it. *He was probably anxious to get out of there before John had come to,* he thought sourly.

Chapter 15

We sat in silence. Silence of speech as freezing gusts continued to hammer the house. It was as if the shrieking winds were testing the very fabric of the structure, puddling around the corners, searching for entry, blowing across the roof, seeking spaces and gaps for access, while we sat huddled in the parlor drinking our tea, the beast pacing ferociously outside.

I wondered at my thoughts and why I felt a malevolence from the storm. *Perhaps because it tried to kill me,* I thought sardonically.

I watched as Gabriel set her teacup down and folded her hands in her lap. When she had saved me from the storm, I had felt her vibrancy and force. Now, she appeared diminished, as if the storm was sucking the very last trickles of life from her. What would I do if there were truly an emergency? What if one of us needed medical care? I prayed that wouldn't happen. We were on our own. No one was coming.

"John was furious," Gabriel said. "He had been cheated out of the workers he had contracted and was left with the weakest of the men and saddled with women and children."

"I'm surprised he didn't leave them there in San Francisco," I said.

Gabriel didn't speak for a moment. She was lost in thought, lost in the diaries. "Yes, it would have been better to leave them all and give up on his gold dreams. He could've had a good life and been a rich man in

San Francisco, but the impressions he had of those golden fields and the lure of easy money as a boy dominated his thoughts. He would never let that go."

"You said he married. Where did he meet her?" I asked.

She gave me a half-smile. "He met her on a train. Her name was Gabby and she lived with her mother, a very poor family from what I understand, but that is getting ahead of ourselves. John and his unlikely group of workers had a hard time ahead of them. He had heard the gold deposits were running dry and more and more miners were returning broke or near to broke, but John had begun to hear stories of gold farther east in the Dakota Territory."

"It's hard to believe he would risk his money on stories," I said.

"Yes, but besides begging as a child, mining gold was all he knew. He was determined to find it no matter what hardships there were or what he had to do. He was driven." She sighed and looked around her. "I believe he had good intentions when he built this place for himself and his wife. He wanted a home and the means to keep it."

I was silent, digesting this. It was beginning to cool in the room, and I knew it was time to add another log to the fire. I rose, my socked feet slippery on the polished floors, and bent down to pick up a log from the settle, carefully setting it on the glowing embers. I watched it flare briefly, feeling the heat on my face as it caught fire. The pieces of rough bark glowed red and then turned to ash as they burned, the dirty gray of the wood reminding me of the storm outside. The storm that would not stop. I was trapped in a house that did not rest easy, with a caretaker who was enmeshed within these walls, and the history of this house.

***

Morning came much too early for John. His head still ached from the day before, and the gold-red streaks across the sky did nothing to help him. He sat up and groaned as the muscles in his back tightened. He wasn't used to sleeping on the ground and preferred a feather bed. He rubbed his eyes and found his unlikely group of workers awake. Bao was cooking the pork and beans while Jin – ah, yes, that was her name – and the other women distributed the food, folded the blankets, and placed them in wicker baskets. He noted this with interest. He had been so angry and frustrated last night that he had paid no attention to the luggage they carried with them. He knew Chinese items brought a fair price, and he would have to investigate this source of revenue. They were brewing tea over the fire, but he would have Bao make him coffee. He had no taste for drinking weeds.

***

John settled in the Pullman car, leaning back into the plush seats as the train pulled away from the depot. Porters still ran frantically up and down the platform, assisting arriving passengers with their heaps of luggage. The engineer pulled the whistle, and John permitted himself a small smile of satisfaction. He had spent less than expected on train passes after explaining his situation in the depot. Even with the reduced rate though, it had cost him over four hundred dollars, but at least the children were free, provided they sat on someone's lap and did not take up room on the third-class benches. He had also spent money on a telegraph to secure his luggage at their destination. Now was the time to review his plans, adjust for shortcomings, and make contingency plans.

He pulled out a small leather-bound notebook and looked around for the waitstaff. He would request a fountain pen. He turned to the aisle, and found himself looking into a very brown set of eyes set off by a rather worn yellow bonnet, her auburn curls escaping the crown and laying on her forehead.

***

Gabriel ceased speaking, and my senses were mesmerized by the fire, watching the climbing flames, my thoughts on John and meeting his betrothed.

Chapter 16

"Gabriel?" I turned to see her chair was empty. Where had she gone? I had not heard her leave. I glanced around the room, knowing there was no place to conceal oneself. My reluctant gaze traveled to the doorway where the stairway could be seen. The door to John's goldmine was open, letting darkness and cold wind its way across the floor. Behind me, the log split, as popping and crackling flames leaped up the fireplace lining, burning shards of wood caught in the creosote.

I froze. I could hear whispers traveling on the darkness from the open door, sliding around the room, icy and sharp, an urgency in the tones. I edged closer to the fire, feeling the heat of the flames, but the cold still chilled as it found me, wrapping around my feet and legs, climbing to my gut where it sat dreadful and frozen. I felt liquid terror in my veins as adrenalin shot through me. The whispers clawed my neck, reaching my ears, whispering, yet I could still not understand. I covered my ears.

"Leave me-me alone!" I cried. My voice was choked and garbled. Still, they pulled at me, slipping between my fingers and settling in my ear canals, frozen talking crystals. I felt the pull of the open door and was terrified to breach that yawning opening. The whispering became louder, insistent. I knew what it wanted. My feet were frozen blocks of ice, unwieldy, as I crossed the floor and stood before the door. I reached up and placed my hands against the wood, a last attempt to prevent myself from entering. I stared at my fingers; the bluish tips were frosted with tiny water drops, and my hands were white as if I had lost all blood. I was a sculpture of ice. Frozen, yet with one purpose – to enter John's mine.

I felt an exhalation pass by me, dirty and damp. The cave was breathing, its malodorous breath raking my face. I stepped across the threshold and found myself at the top of a wooden staircase. Time and use had rimed the treads with piles of wet minerals like sleep-encrusted eyes. I put my hands out to touch the walls and felt slimy protuberances slick under my freezing fingers. I stepped down, testing my weight on the blackened stairs, thinking of all who had passed by on these depressing, mean little steps. Still, the whispers continued, coaxing now, pleading. There was an innocence with these whisps of sound, an innocence laced with nightmares. I could feel its presence, sinuous and rippling under the rocky surface. Waiting. Waiting for someone. Waiting for *me*.

I placed my hand on the wooden railing. Its fibers had long been worn smooth by the grease and sweat of the many hands who had used it decades ago. I began my descent step by treacherous step. The staircase twisted back on itself like nonfunctioning DNA, its gene pool contaminated until only a murky glow came from above.

I reached the bottom and wished for the flashlight on my phone that was now submerged in an icy drift. The opening to the cave yawned before me; the darkness absolute, a Vantablack, absorbing ninety-nine percent of the light. I hesitated, my stockinged feet feeling the moistness of the dirt on the stone. I could hear the drip, drip of water further down the cave, and the musty, moldy smell of stagnant water and organic material assaulted my nostrils. Yet, still, the whispers came. Louder now. Imploring me forward. I moved ahead, my toes shuffling through the dirt and pebbles. The memory of my dirty, bloody sheets and the soreness of my feet flashed through my mind.

What was I doing? I thought. *Why did I care about these voices in the dark?* I needed to turn and go back up those melancholic, joyless stairs and wait. Wait for the godforsaken snow to stop. Wait for rescue. Leave this place with Gabriel. Surely, I could convince her to leave. I swiveled on my feet, feeling stones pierce through my socks, then I reached for the slick railing, and froze as the door above me slammed shut. I could feel the reverberation through the handrail. The darkness was now complete. Teeth chewed the sides of my stomach as I felt the cave's putrid breath slip by me. I gagged and felt my belly tighten. Clinging to the wood, I stretched my foot, searching for the lowest step. *Where in the hell was that step?*

"*Gabriel*," I whispered. I was alone. Alone in this stygian dark. One wrong move and I would surely drop into an abyss. The overwhelming darkness of the cave. The stinking claustrophobia of the cave. I felt the hot froth of hysteria course through my body. I would lose control. I would fall into a shaft and lay there dead or wounded. No one would come. There was no one to care. Breathless sounds echoed around me, and I fought to keep screams from erupting from my tightened throat. I let go of the slippery rail, covered my shaking mouth, and then realized it was my panting, terrified breathing echoing back to me a hundred times, bouncing off the concavity of the tunnel mercilessly as it threw my panic back at me.

I breathed through my nose, focusing on my lungs, in... out... in... out. The cave breathed with me from hundreds of little orifices, little mouths attached to never ending tracheas branching out and then coalescing into a version of malformed lungs.

I was going to die down here.

My mouth opened, and my lungs filled, as hysteria rose and then stopped as my hands left my mouth. Was my brain playing tricks on me? Wanting desperately to see something, anything; just filling in the blanks? I leaned slightly toward the gloom. Surely, I was seeing a source of incandescence. I stepped closer to the wall and held up my hand. A sickly shadow, four fingers, and a thumb cast a weak pall on the wall. Which meant – I whirled to look behind me, feeling my breath leave my body as I stared into the darkness – a shifting of shadows. Black muddied color with amorphous grays moved in the depths of the tunnel. My eyes widened, trying to decipher – to make sense of what I saw. I did not want to enter the tunnel, but still, the whispers entreated me forward. I gave one final look up the serpentine stairway and saw nothing but darkness, and then I turned to enter the oval shape cut into the rock tonnage above me.

I shuffled my feet forward, my hands on the slick walls of the narrow tunnel. The noise from my tread tricked my ears, and I turned to look behind me, feeling the tense muscles in my neck protest, certain something followed, but there was nothing.

I traveled for what seemed like a distance. One hesitating footstep after another. I knew that the tunnels of South Dakota stretched for miles, and there were many unknown, unexplored passageways. *Was I in one of those?* I thought. I felt a frisson of unease pass down my back at the thought of losing my way and endlessly wandering these dark holes. I knew I had not passed any other passageways as I had kept both hands stretched to the damp, slippery walls. *But are you certain?* I thought. I tried to dismiss the panic those thoughts aroused and focused on the undulating glow that still seemed just out of reach – the long hallway in dreams where you never quite reach the end.

Except the end of the tunnel came suddenly. One moment, my hands trailed the rocky, wet walls, and the next, I stood alone on what felt like a precipice with no support from the stones. I think it was a room, a cavern, which is what spelunkers called it, and I wondered, in this time of stress, why it mattered that I should label the structure. Perhaps it was my mind protecting itself against the panic and terror I felt.

This cavern was the source of light that had drawn me down the long passageway. I could see darker entryways lining the circumference and wondered at their stories. I could hear the drip, drip leaving the ceiling and little splashes as they formed pools of water on the floor. Concavities and convexities made up the rocky walls, and little beads of water glowed like crystals, fusing as they descended, forming little arteries bleeding onto the floor.

The pleading whispers had not stopped as I journeyed down the tunnel, and now the gibbosity of sound was all around me. I couldn't tell if it was one voice or a thousand as the fusillade of aches surrounded me.

"I can't understand you!" I cried. The loneliness and fear of the voices were like mourning doves, their melancholy cries enough to prick your heart.

"I want to help..." My voice died away as I sensed an animus, a hostility, enter the rocky enclosure. Its discordant tones scattered the plaintive voices, and my breath caught in my throat.

There was good, and there was evil.

Evil had entered the hollow.

My sodden feet worked backward toward the path of the rickety stairs. The sad little voices would have to wait; I wasn't brave enough, didn't care enough, to stay here with the threat of – *threat of what?* I wondered. There was nothing I could see save the odd glow, and even that might be explained by some strange bioluminescence. Even as I attempted to reason with myself, I noticed something. Something on the cave floor, where dirt met stone. A crevice or gap... something did not make sense to my eyes. As I gazed upon it, the shadows moved, and I gasped and stepped back, fumbling for the exit from which I had come. The ground was slippery, and I stumbled, my head made contact with the rocks strewn about the floor. I sat up with a groan, feeling the cave shift, as if on a see-saw, that gradually rights itself. I looked about in a haze of pain, momentarily forgetting the shifting darkness, but then I was brutally reminded as the shadows leaped up the cavern's walls, filling in little pits and holes and gliding over gravelly surfaces.

It was a dance, a dance that smoothed the walls with black ink, making impossible jumps from rock to rock. I sat on the earth, feeling the stones and pebbles dig into my hands and legs. I was awake, I was aware, this was happening before my eyes. The more they moved, the more I began to feel a purpose in these slivers of black. Arms and legs began to form, a muddled head and suggestions of hair.

Unlike the allegory of the cave, there was no fire here, and I would turn to see the source. I rose, still dizzy from my fall, and turned. There was nothing. No light source, no playful figures. I whirled back to the wall. The shadows still played, and yet I cast no darkness.

These lovely, playful shadow children moved across the wall. Their arms intertwining to become one and then disentangling to weave with another. They played like all children played, bringing a smile to my lips. They grew and evolved, flourishing across the wall, as I sat enraptured by their essence, and yet a shiver crossed my neck. As if a reptile slithered across the floor that had been there all along.

Its darkness rose along the wall, engulfing the children's shades. They became hunched and jagged. There was no more playful plaiting and knitting. Instead, they ruptured and scattered across the wall, and still the serpent rose, but now it appeared to be undulating as if a tsunami hit the walls, drowning the children, their arms frantic above their heads. I could see mouths open, and my head was filled with their cries for help... but I could not help them.

I cried out for it to stop, and shockingly, the shadow turned toward me as I sat unprotected on the floor. It gathered the shades of the children in its arms, and it lurched at me. Shadow pieces of the children fell to the floor until there were just bones – beautiful, fragile bones in its arms.

"Rachael!" Gabriel screamed from the tunnel, shock and horror written on her face.

I gasped, my head swiveling to take in her appearance. She was so delicate, so small in the entryway. I feared for her, this lonely little woman.

"Gabriel, go back!" I cried. She stood frozen, a chrysalis in ice, her eyes fixed on the revolting mess that held the shards of mortality.

"Get back, John!" Gabriel's voice had deepened in timbre, its echo racing around the cavern, seeming to pick up speed as it assaulted my eardrums.

I gaped at her and then cut my gaze to the entity. It had stilled its course; little black ripples caressing the helpless ivory bones in its arms.

It appeared to deepen and darken, its torso? My mind screamed in denial. It was taking shape, seeming to absorb the vestiges of the shadow children; their screaming, helpless cries tearing at my head and my heart. If only I could help them, protect them. Gabriel's low tones continued to command and fight, pushing it back further to the wall. In one last glut, the thing rose to the ceiling, taking all air with it, leaving me gasping and clawing for precious oxygen, and then it exhaled a tsunami of decay and age, leaving me retching on the floor. I sat back on my heels, wiping my mouth and streaming eyes. Little shadows, a thousand little snakes writhed on the floor, disappearing into fissures and cracks in the rocks and dirt.

I stumbled to my feet and met Gabriel at the tunnel.

Chapter 17

My arm was around Gabriel's waste as we struggled up the stairs. She had her hand on the railing that glistened from the dampness of the cave. The open door from above cast a weak light down through the wooden slats of the twisted staircase, enabling us to keep our footing. My knees were weak, and I was breathing heavily from shock; in contrast, I could scarcely hear Gabriel's breath. Her limbs were so light, they were almost birdlike, and I wondered at her ability to help me from the snow when I first arrived. The only task I believed she was capable of now was holding a teacup and a lace-edged napkin.

"Try to hurry, Gabriel," I implored her. I hated rushing her but did not want to spend a second longer in that horrifying cave. Even now, the repugnant smell of decay washed up on us, making me cough. I fought to keep my empty stomach from twisting, my mouth still sour and foul-tasting from vomiting on the cave floor.

When would this nightmare end?

***

I had settled Gabriel in a chair by the fire and stepped quickly back to the parlor door, slamming it shut. It rattled in its frame, and I paused, wondering if it would spring open again. It held, and I turned back to the fragile woman. Her head was bowed, her hair shining with a silvery nimbus from the weak firelight. She looked like an aging angel, and I felt a rush of concern and fear for her. It wasn't right that she should be here by herself. In what reality did the owners of this hotel think this was appropriate?

I added wood to the fire and watched the flames rise, and I held my hands out, watching as the fire outlined them in orange and gold. Then, I turned from the warmth and dragged my chair closer to hers.

"Gabriel?" I asked. She slowly raised her head. Her papery skin skimmed over her face, allowing me to see the delicate bone structure beneath. I shuddered remembering the scraps of mortality the abhorrent – was it John? – thing had held in its appendages.

"Gabriel, what was that-that downstairs?" She was still silent. "Was that, John, Gabriel?" I persisted. She did not reply, but I saw her frail shoulders move slightly.

"John haunts this house," I said. A statement. An unbelievable statement. I had come looking for a ghostly presence to entertain my readers and found this-this monstrosity, but who would believe me if they had not experienced it? I was here, and I found it hard to believe; hard to believe I hadn't hallucinated it, and yet Gabriel was here, and she had experienced the same.

"Gabriel." Her gaze had wandered, and I wanted to bring her back to the present, back to me. This time, her eyes immediately found mine. "Were those children down there? The shadows on the wall? Were those John's children?"

Her breath released in a huff. "No, no, not John's. He and his wife were barren. Yes, they were children, precious children."

"What happened to them? Did John..." I paused, afraid to say the words. "Did he hurt them in some way?"

She looked at me with such heartbreak and sadness that I wanted to weep. "Gabriel..."

She held up her hand. "You need to know how it came to pass."

***

The girl's name was Gabby Winston. She was returning to Council Bluffs, Iowa, after helping her grandmother make the difficult transition from two to one. Her grandmother and grandfather had owned and run a small cafe on the San Francisco Bay, but now Elizabeth was alone as her husband had passed away. She had sent for Gabby, paid her train fare, and fed her while she was there helping her get another girl trained. Gabby's mother was more than willing to let Gabby go. She had five other children, with Gabby being the eldest, and she was, as yet, unmarried. Her mother hoped but did not expressly tell Gabby to find a man to take care of her in California, thereby ridding herself of the extra mouth to feed. Unfortunately, or fortunately, that had not happened. Elizabeth had kept Gabby on her feet from dawn until night working at the cafe, and although she did meet men who had complimented her looks and manners while serving them hot meals and coffee, none were interested in matrimony.

So, she was returning to Iowa with very little money that Elizabeth had begrudgingly paid her and no husband. She turned to look out the train window. A line of Chinese men, women, and children were making their way down the platform to what she presumed were the cargo cars. Her mother had sent her to California, paying the cheapest rate, and she had found herself sitting on a bench for two days.

Other females had been present but not with the backgrounds she was accustomed to, so she had not engaged with them. She did find unlikely comradery with the Chinese, especially the children, with their almond-shaped eyes and deep black hair. She had learned a few Chinese words, too, and had practiced them with the women, much to their mutual amusement. When her food had ran out, they had shared their rice dishes with her. That train ride had been the highlight of her visit to her grandmother. She wished she could be back there with the Chinese now, learning their names and playing with the children, but her grandmother had insisted she use her wages and pay for the first-class carriage. Gabby knew she did not want her granddaughter to appear in Iowa, descending from the cargo car.

She mentally shrugged her shoulders. No matter, she knew the minute she arrived, her mother would take any money left in her purse, so she might as well relax and enjoy the unexpected luxury of being waited upon instead of doing the waiting.

She continued watching out her window. The din was loud and boisterous. The city had so much movement and life, with new ships arriving daily. People from all over the world came to this little bay, hoping to make their fortunes in Sutter's gold fields. She had heard talk from the men that gold was becoming scarce, and miners competing with each other over claims would come to blows or worse. Resentment was building against the Chinese as they worked over abandoned claims and, through careful and tedious work, found more gold in these deserted areas. As gold sources dwindled and employment became scarce, President Arthur signed the Chinese Exclusion Act to prevent more immigration of Chinese workers. She admired the Chinese. How brave they must be to come halfway around the world to America, leaving difficult living conditions at home in search of their fortune.

A booming male voice caught her attention, and she searched for the source. Ah – there he was. He stood just behind the large group of Chinese people she had been watching. He attempted to herd them toward the freight cars, but they appeared confused and frightened. The children were crying, and the men and women were carrying luggage, and thus unable to pick them up and comfort them. She considered vacating her seat in the Pullman car to assist the bellowing man and the bewildered group. As she watched, a porter reached them and guided the group back to where they had been assigned, and the man took off his hat and rubbed his face. The sun picked out highlights in his brown hair, and sweat made deep v-marks on his linen shirt. He was tall and broad-shouldered, and she could hear the thumping of his dusty boots even over the sweltering noise of the passengers and luggage carts.

She knew he must be one of the miners who employed the Chinese to dig his claims and wondered why the women and children were part of the group. Surely, he would not use them in the minefields. Her curiosity was not satisfied as they walked further down the platform and out of her sight.

***

The girl had piqued John's interest, and he watched her as she surreptitiously took small glances at him. Whenever she caught his eye, a light rose blush would cover her cheeks and make him smile. He wondered at the worn bonnet and dress and the expense of the first-class ticket. She wore no ring and did not seem to be accompanied by anyone. The waitstaff had taken a liking to her, he had noticed with irritation, and she responded with grateful sounds and smiles.

He rose and walked to his sleeping car, intent on washing and donning clean clothes. He was going to talk to her.

***

The great, sweaty man had disappeared, and she felt slightly disappointed. Perhaps he had caught her looking at him, becoming irritated or embarrassed at her silly glances. No matter, she would enjoy the train ride, knowing it was all too short, and she would be back home facing the drudgery of home life with five brothers and sisters to care for and no prospects of ever leaving. She looked out the window and watched the landscape, trying to imprint the desolate, extraordinary scenery into her memories.

"Hello, miss?" She turned to find the man of her previous attentions standing before her, smiling down at her.

"I was wondering if I might join you?" he continued and, without her permission, sat down.

"My name is John Hawthorne."

***

Before the train had arrived in Council Bluffs, Gabby was in love. In love with his tales of gold, in love with his stature and strength. Her heart beat faster when he regaled her with stories from his past, his humble upbringing, to the success he was today. He talked to her about the Dakota Territory and his hopes of finding gold. They spoke of the passing landscape, the wildlife, and the train itself.

"I've never sat on velvet cushions before," Gabby said. Her ungloved hand stroked the soft green fabric. "In fact, I've never been waited on before. I have always done the waiting, the cleaning, and cooking." A sound caught her attention, and she watched a very fine lady sitting a few tables down from them. Her tinkling laugh was as delightful as the flute of champagne she sipped. Gabby reached for her own crystal goblet and sipped, the sharp effervescence making her want to sneeze. She plucked a strawberry from a cut glass bowl and lifted her gaze to the polished woodwork, the intricately carved flowers making her marvel. Then, she glimpsed her reflection in one of the gilt mirrors that lined the car and felt ashamed to be seen in such a rich, lavishly decorated environment. Her threadbare bonnet and old gown were so dowdy. She leaned closer and found reflection upon reflection staring back at her. Opposing mirrors were hung on each side of the car, reflecting endlessly; each iteration of Gabby's drab bonnet slowly fading until just a shade of yellow outlined a pale face, the drabness of her bonnet disappearing as if she might one day be one of those elegant ladies that laughed so carelessly.

She couldn't imagine what a gentleman like John Hawthorne saw in her. Perhaps he felt sorry for her that she traveled alone.

She felt his eyes upon her and found him looking at her consideringly. "There is nothing wrong with women's work and taking pride in it." A soft rose color appeared on her cheeks. He liked to see the color and know he was the one who caused it. "Yes, first-class cars are very luxurious, aren't they?" He didn't wait for her answer and continued. "I would have been mighty interested in watching the last spike driven into the railroad ties. It was about fourteen ounces in gold copper alloy. They used a special silver hammer to drive it home. I bet it was real pretty."

"How will you know where to look for the gold once you reach the territory?" Gabby asked. She was eager to learn all about John and his plans, knowing they would soon part and she would be back at home, unable to escape. She wanted these memories to last a lifetime.

He smiled at her, enjoying the attention. "I started panning for gold when I was a boy. I don't know if you're familiar with the Black Hills Expedition?" She shook her head. "It was an expedition led by Custer to find locations for a fort and..." he paused, "gold."

She breathed in excitement. "I know you will find gold! What an adventure you are on!"

He smiled at her, appreciating the admiration in her eyes.

"Who will be helping you?" Gabby asked.

His smile vanished, leaving a coldness to him that made her shiver, as he looked at the passing grasses out the window. "I've paid for some Chinese workers," he said sourly.

She frowned, her forehead wrinkling, as she had not meant to upset him. "I'm sorry. I've heard they're very good workers. I believe I saw your group when you were boarding the train. They looked to be a good, hard-working group," she said, hoping to please him.

He shrugged his shoulders. "The men, perhaps, but I hadn't counted on being stuck with a passel of women and children. However, due to an unfortunate event, well, here I am, and so are they." He flicked his finger at the porter, indicating another whisky. The alcohol was an inferior brand to the one he had filched from the barkeep, but he was saving that for his arrival in the Dakota Territory.

She considered this. "When I was sent to California to help my grandmother, I traveled in the cargo car," she said. She felt embarrassed to admit this but wanted to lift his spirits regarding his Chinese workers, women and children included. "They were very pleasant to me. The women were happy and helpful; they even shared their food when I-I had run out," she finished, her face flaming.

He looked at her aghast. "My dear Gabby." He reached across the table to capture her hand that fluttered about with her lace-edged handkerchief. "It's criminal that you were placed in that car. Surely your parents?" He stopped, not wanting to insult her or them.

"Travel expenses for first or even second-class were quite out of the question," she said. "I am traveling here in this car with money I had saved working for my grandmother. The rest will be turned over to my mother when I arrive. It's terribly decadent of me, of course, but my grandmother—"

She shrugged her shoulders and looked down at their entwined hands.

"My dear girl," he said, reaching across the table to cup her chin to look into her eyes. "This is sudden and you do not have to answer me yet, but your excitement for my way of life, your sense of adventure, stirs me. Would you do me the great honor of becoming my wife?"

Gabby looked at him, stunned he should offer such a thing to her. It was an unusual proposal, not what she had ever dreamed it would be, but what did he offer? A chance to leave home, to shake off the dust of her mother, escape the drudgery of home life... without another moment's thought, she replied, "Yes."

***

When they arrived in Council Bluffs, there was the same confusion, voices, and activity they had experienced in San Francisco. The porters calling to each other, the thump of trunks and cases landing on the platform, the shouts of loved ones welcoming home their own, the dirt and grit in the air. Gabby stepped down onto the platform, John holding her elbow. The steam engine's smell of oily smoke and moisture wafted over them, but it didn't matter to Gabby; she reveled in all of it knowing this was not her last stop. She would be traveling with John to exciting new places, new land, and new adventures.

"Ho George!" John called out. One of the porters near them swiveled on the heel and came trotting over to them.

"May I help you, sir?" the young black man asked.

"Yes, boy. I have a load of Chinese back in the freight car, and I need them brought up to me," John said.

"Yes, sir," he said, turning, and making a circuitous route through the melee of people and luggage.

"Do you know him?" Gabby asked. It was uncomfortable on the platform. The sun was hot on her head, and she could feel sweat gathering on her brow and neck. She could see other ladies with embroidered, lacy parasols looking cool and untroubled, their escorts holding valises. Carriages stood ready at the depot in anticipation of removing the beautiful people from the sweaty dirtiness and depositing them safely behind painted white doors and chilled marble floors. Handsome horses moved their heads, causing their harnesses to jingle as their coachman spoke to them, their brushed, silky tails flicking at flies.

John looked down at her in surprise. "No, I do not. They're all called George, or boy. They're the George Pullman boys. Named after George's Pullman sleeping car. Hey, boy!" John raised his arm at the George he had summoned earlier, as the boy led the group of bedraggled Chinese through the maze of confusion. John clicked his tongue in impatience as the boy stopped to pick up a screaming Chinese child. The woman, presumably the mother, tried to take the child back, fear on her face, but then the worried, tired lines disappeared as the child ceased crying to touch the boy's face. Damn, what he wouldn't do to be rid of the women and children.

The disheveled group arrived to stand in front of John and Gabby. The men wore conical rattan hats pulled low over their foreheads, and the women were bare-headed; their long, silky hair pulled back and fastened with ivory sticks. Their clothes were loose fitting, almost childlike in fashion, precluding ornamentation over function. The children wore tiny garments, copies of their parents'. They were shy as they hid behind the adults, their faces showing little circles of dirt where they had sweated and then gotten dusty from the train. They all stared at him. Uneasy. Uncertain of their future.

John looked over the motley group and shook his head, as thoughts of leaving them all behind passed through his mind again, but he knew time was of the essence. The stories of gold in the Dakota Territory would bring hundreds of hopeful miners, intent on finding their fortunes. He cast about him, his mind searching for alternatives, and alighted on the porters, the Georges, the boys; however they were not an option either. He had heard they were paid a pittance, less than a dollar a day if his sources were to be believed. John would not pay that, and he couldn't imagine they would consider leaving their comfortable, clean work situation to travel hundreds of miles to dig in the hills.

"Is everything all right, John?" Gabby asked, and John turned to her, his face softening momentarily. Here was a partner, someone who could help him with the Chinese. Keep the children out of the way, and the women working.

"No, darling," he replied, "everything is fine."

***

Gabriel had fallen silent, her voice dwindling as she described the woman on the train. The caretaker was shrinking before my eyes, closing in on herself as if each word of John's life was strangling her life force and soon she would be a mere husk.

I needed to get her – to get us – out of here. I rose from the chair and went to the window, pulling the draperies back. Frost had made fantastical swirls on the glass panes. I placed my hand upon the icy window, letting the warmth of my hand thaw the icy particles, and I shivered as I felt the dampness of the cold water. I wiped the moisture on my clothes as I peered through the skeletal handprint.

The murky twilight made it difficult to distinguish land from sky, as the storm still pummeled the landscape. Murmurations of snow and ice twisted and folded into uncanny shapes, and I felt the familiar clenching of my stomach and tightening of my throat. There was something horribly wrong with this house... I turned from the window to look back at the woman... and with Gabriel.

Chapter 18

I returned to my chair and sat down, reaching out to the fire to warm my frozen hands. I could sense Gabriel stirring and turned to see her gaze on me. Little twin flames reflected in her eyes, those tiny glimmers the only signs of life on her face.

I felt my breath leave my lungs, my heart hammering.

"Gabriel, are you all right?" I asked, my voice strangled.

Her head slowly fell to one side and came to rest on her shoulder, her neck at an impossible angle. The tightened muscles in her neck snaked up her throat, the shadows cast by the firelight making deep lacerations. The light from the fire gave her eyes movement, and they appeared to watch me, darting about my face.

"Gabriel!" My voice had risen, frightened at her visage. I rose to shake her, to stop those terrifying eye movements, and then I froze, as her mouth had slowly opened, hanging as if she had no control over her musculature. A thin line of spittle began to form at the corner of her mouth, tracing a dark line to her chin and disappearing into the tendons in her neck.

I stood, and then was unable to move. Perhaps she was having a heart attack? A stroke? I had no medical training. No way to help her. I felt hysteria rising like hot bubbles in my chest.

Then, the true terror began.

Suggestions of sound, whispers, light, and dancing filled the room's corners, seeping like a stain onto the floorboards, creeping along the burnished wood as they met under Gabriel's chair.

I stumbled back as the horrifying shadows rose to encircle the chair legs where she still sat, her mouth hanging, her eyes twin points of light, still fixed on me.

"Gabriel!" I cried. The backs of my legs hit my chair, and I whirled, startled at the sudden touch. I pushed the chair back as I turned to keep my eyes on the creeping mass that had now climbed to engulf her torso and neck.

All attempts at helping Gabriel fled my mind, and my terror sent me to the door, intending to fling it open and take my chances in the storm.

I ran across the room, my feet slipping on the glossy floors, hitting the door's surface, as I groped for the handle. My hands were suddenly sweaty with fright, as I pulled at the door knob. It twisted in my grip, not giving way. I yanked and pushed, and still, it refused to open. My knees were weak with adrenalin as I pounded my fists, bruising.

"Let me out!" I screamed. My pulse thumped in my ears; I was panting and felt moisture on my face. Was I crying? Even over my sounds of fear and panic, I could hear the sliding whispers gather in strength, their agitated breathing matching my own.

I turned to face the awful maelstrom of sound. The crawling darkness had utterly engulfed Gabriel, leaving a pasty white circle around her open mouth. As I watched in horrified fascination, the shadowy particles slipped into her mouth. The whispers began to get louder, as if her voice gave these fragile slips of darkness access to vocal cords, to speech... a way to communicate.

I fumbled behind me, trying to open the door, but it still refused to give way.

Giving one last futile yank on the door knob, I turned to her and screamed, "Gabriel, help me!"

The whispers rose to shrieks and echoed my words. "Help me! Help me!" Her mouth made tremulous, jerky movements as the words left her.

Dear God, was she a prisoner in her own body, held by this-this malevolence?

I stepped across the room, my legs stiff with fear, and my arms wrapped around my torso. The fire still burned, but no heat came from that quarter. I could see the mist of my breath leading me to the woman, as I reached her chair and put my hand out to her. My fingers were shaking and icy, like icicles hanging at the end of my arms. I looked into her eyes and saw pure terror. She was in there and needed help. My help.

"Gabriel," I said, lightly touching her shoulder. I felt the hard surface of bone beneath the material of her dress. She was so thin. The whispers had diminished, and I felt emboldened and touched her cheek, the texture like rice paper.

"Gabriel," I whispered. Small sounds came from her trembling lips, and I leaned closer. "Tell me how to help you." I bent closer, my ear to her mouth, trying to hear, trying to help. I could feel the cold moisture from her mouth, cooling my ear and cheek, and inhaled the foulness of rot.

"Help us, Rachael."

I jerked back from her mouth, standing shocked at what I heard, tremors shaking my body, but even as I processed the words, the shadows were leaving Gabriel and encircling her, encircling me.

The shadow children of the cave.

I stood with my back to Gabriel's chair, her mouth agape, the putrescent smell surrounding her forlorn little body, and I watched these darkling figures.

They waxed and waned about us, ebbing and flowing. Their darkness would gather like a vortex and then scatter only to interfuse once again. These little things. These dancing forms; their shadowed limbs ending in wispy bits of darkness, their hair flowing like ink to the floor, swirling around gloomy faces with darkened eye concavities, nostrils expanding and decreasing with each breath, open mouths imploring me to help them.

I was drawn to them and repelled. Wanting to help, but how? I was certain I was going to die in this house.

I heard Gabriel stir behind me and turned to her. Her eyes blinked slowly, trying to focus. I bent down, relieved she was still with me and happy to notice the smell had dissipated.

"They need protection, Rachael," she whispered.

"From who? From what?" I said savagely. "This isn't my problem. When the snow clears, I'm out of here – with or without you."

I turned and left the room... away from that infuriating pity I saw in her eyes, noting the damned door now opened easily.

Chapter 19

I sat on my creaking bed with the quilt wrapped around me, trying to warm my shivering body. I had traveled here hoping to find a frothy, entertaining story, and instead I had found a claustrophobic nightmare buried under a snowstorm that would not cease, atop suffocating labyrinthine caves.

I looked across the room to the window. The panes were completely frosted over, with water crystals sparkling in the dim light. I could hear Gabriel's movements downstairs. She scared me almost as much as the children, and if she was to be believed, John's presence.

What did I believe? Were there ghosts in the night? Spirits that were anchored to places or people? Before embarking on this journey, I had researched these very things, and I knew some felt ghosts were as casually present as getting a cup of coffee each day. Others had recorded their experiences and were terrified at the happenings. I strongly sided with them.

Gabriel had intimated that John had something to do with the children. Those little shades of humanity. Shadow children. Shadow people. This assignment led me to investigate these beings and find their beginnings in the Native Americans and Islam. Some believed they were benign; others felt they were demons or aliens set on harming the observer. I had rolled my eyes at this but dutifully made notes.

Notes that were buried under the snow. I cast my eyes over to the window. We were in a perpetual state of the blue hour. Never quite day, never quite night.

What else had I learned about the shadow people? Some believed they were people from another dimension and could be seen where the fabric of time and space was thin. Many sightings occurred during sleep paralysis, where the prone observer lay helpless while the shadow person menaced them. I shivered despite the warmth of the quilt. That would be terrifying. I was very glad that I had never experienced sleep paralysis, never mind the sideshow of shadow people.

In all my research, the shadow people were stationary, with no movement, no sound – products of a malfunctioning brain or terrified imagination – whereas these little shades of the underground moved; they danced and had a voice. Furthermore, I was not asleep.

"Rachael!" I gasped as Gabriel called from the bottom of the stairs, stairs that guarded John's Dark Paradise.

What of Gabriel? When she first rescued me from the snow, she appeared vibrant; strong enough to pluck me from my icy enclosure, but now... now she appeared barely strong enough to hold her teacup. Her physical self had deteriorated to the point where, if we were in a city, she would be in the hospital, hooked up to machines and attended by caring nurses and doctors, not in this hell hole of a house out in the hills.

There were prickles of thought that teased the outer edges of my brain. Thoughts of Gabriel's presence here, and her connection to Hawthorne House. I couldn't allow myself to go down that road, or I would lose my mind and run out into the storm, heedless of what would be certain death. I had to accept her as she portrayed herself: a lonely caretaker with a ghost problem.

"Rachael!" she called again. I shuddered, and standing, went downstairs to meet her.

***

Gabriel sat at the kitchen table, the ever-present teacup in her hands, her skin almost as translucent as the bone china.

"I need answers, Gabriel," I said, sitting down on the kitchen chair with a thump and holding up my hand to negate her offer of tea.

"What is happening here? What does John have to do with it? What did he do to the kids?" My tone was waspish. I did not care that she looked ready to fall over. My sanity was slipping.

"I'm sorry, Rachael. This was not what I had planned, not what I wanted. You are so young." She sighed and put down her teacup.

"What do you mean by that?" I said, infuriated by her oblique answers.

"Let me finish the story—"

"I am sick of John's story. He was an asshole from all accounts. I want to know what those shadows are! Why are they asking for help? What is that-that thing in the caves? No more stories!" I finished, breathing heavily.

She gazed at me with more life in her eyes than I had seen in a while. "I will finish, and you will get all your questions answered, but it will be *my* way. Besides, Rachael," she turned to look out the kitchen window, where the snow beat against the panes and the wind howled, "you're not going *anywhere*."

***

They were to travel to a boarding house for the next few days while John and his foreman, Bao, finished preparations for the journey ahead. They rode in a wagon, with the Chinese walking alongside. The heat was sweltering, and Gabby had pitied them. Their feet scuffed up dirt as fine as powder and settled on their cotton slippers, turning them brown. The children had long since given up, and the adults held them as they walked, their little faces burning in the sun and moist with perspiration.

"John, can we let them ride on the wagons, surely—"

"No," he replied. He was distracted as they arrived in Council Bluffs. It was a bustling city full of horses, wagons, and people. Abe Lincoln had declared it the eastern terminus of the transcontinental railroad, and it had become known as the Gateway to the American West.

John wanted to show Gabby a special place. Something that he had heard about and dreamed of when he began planning his gold-mining expedition. It was a house. A house that would befit a man of his substance and soon-to-be-realized wealth. A house that would shelter him and his heirs.

"I have a surprise for you." He turned to her and was puzzled to see her brow puckered; her mouth turned down. He had already forgotten her request to let the Chinese ride.

"Yes?" she asked. "What is it?" Her long-sleeved jacket was sweltering, and she could hardly bear the heat, even with the loosening of the cuffs. Her skirts hung in dismal swaths of fabric. She felt dirty and exhausted and could only imagine how horrible it must be for those walking.

"Be patient. I believe it is just up ahead," he said. He had pulled an envelope from his pocket and consulted the crudely drawn map. "Yes, it is," he added, replacing it and flicking the horses with his whip. They trotted faster, and while she was grateful for the air's movement, the increased pace forced the Chinese to move more quickly.

"John—"

"Ah – there it is!" He pointed to a house – a mansion. Gabby followed his finger and saw Grenville Dodge's home. It was no surprise to her; after all, she lived here and had viewed the house from afar as she grew up in the area.

"It's much bigger than what I'd thought!" he said. She watched him as his eyes devoured the home, then he pulled out his square fat pencil notebook and began making notes. The horses moved uneasily, and he snapped at them and continued to study the house.

"What are you doing, John?" she asked. She didn't understand his delight in the home. Yes, it was beautiful. Yes, it was opulent, but what did it have to do with them? With him and his dreams of gold?

He continued to write, his pencil scratching the paper, the noise irritating like the sounds of the flies that found her and buzzed mercilessly about her sweating face as they sat motionless, waiting.

He snapped his notebook closed, causing her to jump, and he laid a hand on her arm. "That, my love," he pointed to the house, "will be our home. Well..." he amended, "not this mansion, but we will build one once we reach the Dakota Territory. It will be built out of wood... but no matter. The style is French, did you know?" He went on without waiting for her answer. "The roof is mansard. I doubt I will be able to copy that but we will have the dormers and the pavilion porch, eh? You can walk the porch, drink lemonade, and wait for your husband to return home." He did not look at her but continued to study the building – his thoughts on the magnificence of the structure and how he would come to make one for himself.

Neighing from the horses pulled him out of his reverie, and he turned from the house and flicked the reins. Gabby was relieved to see them settle into an easy walk. She looked back at the Chinese group, some of the children had woken up and began to fuss and cry. John also heard it and glanced back; his eyebrows sinking, and his mouth tightening.

He yanked the horses to a standstill, they whinnied, and their front feet rose.

"Down!" John cried, and they settled, prancing nervously. "Get out," he commanded Gabby." Get them some water from the barrel and put the brats in the wagon. I'll not let them hold me up."

She glanced at him in surprise. The warm brown eyes that glowed when he talked of his plans were cold now, the golden light frozen. She shivered despite the heat and got off the wagon, almost falling in her haste. When she looked back at him, he had already pulled his notebook out, scratching the pages with his pencil.

She hurried back to the group, her skirts damp from sitting so long, sticking to her and chafing her backside. She turned to the wagon with the water and rummaged in a wooden box for tin cups. After locating them, she opened the barrel cork, filled a bucket, and set it on the dusty ground. She had spilled water over the side in her rush to get them water, and it disappeared instantly, the dry dirt as thirsty as the ones who walked on it.

She motioned to them and mimed drinking. The children came first, running to get their drinks; the adults following, letting them drink their fill.

"Gabby!"

She turned to see John standing on the wagon, his hands on his hips. He reminded her of the first day she saw him on the train platform in San Francisco. He was larger than life that day. Such a great man. A strong man. How unnerving and exciting it had been when he had shown interest in her. She felt a trickle of unease as she noted his impatience with her and his contempt for the Chinese. Surely, things would improve once they began their journey and his dreams were realized.

***

John had arranged for the Chinese to stay at a boarding house while he and Gabby traveled together to meet her parents and receive their blessing. It had been difficult for him to find lodging for the Chinese in Council Bluffs, but he eventually learned of a house that would accept them. Lodgings from reputable boarding houses were out of the question. They would not accept any boarders except Americans and were thirty-five cents a night. He settled on one costing just ten cents a night with no board. One room would house ten adults, so he had reserved two, and they could determine who would sleep where. It made no difference to him. He would let Bao take care of it.

He and Gabby pulled away from the boarding house. They would sleep in a much finer place, but first, they would meet her mother.

***

Gabby directed him through the darkened roads. The sun was setting, and she hoped the twilight would hide the house's many shortcomings. She could feel embarrassment clenching at her throat. Her family lived in a small two-room house with space above for sleeping. The outside walls were rough, with unfinished planks stuffed with grass and mud to prevent the elements from seeping in. It was laughable next to John's dreams of a house like General Dodge. She wished she could plead that it did not matter if he received her mother's blessing. She would go with him. Go anywhere as long as she escaped the poverty and drudgery that was her life, but even in the little time she had come to know him, she knew there would be no changing his mind. She recognized the coldness of his eyes and the way his jaw set when he was determined or angry. She wished she could transport them to the Dakota Territory, happy in their new house and enough gold to make John happy. She wished—

"Gabby!" She was jerked from her reverie, almost painfully, as a young voice brought her to the present. It was her little sister, happy to see her.

"Lizzy! Hello, it's good to see you," she cried, and it was... until she saw the young girl through John's eyes. Dirty feet, scuffling in the dirt, her face and hands grimy. Snarling hair wound its way across her scalp, and she held a scrawny cat in her arms. She must have squeezed the cat too hard in her excitement, and it yowled and leaped from her arms, leaving a bleeding scratch on her forearm. Lizzy began to scream, and Gabby jumped from the wagon, feeling John's censure weighing her back. She knelt before the girl and took her in her arms. Calming her and taking her handkerchief from her skirt, she wiped the blood, and then kissed her forehead.

"Where's Ma?" Gabby asked.

"In-inside," Lizzy replied, hiccupping as the last sobs disappeared.

"All right, then," Gabby said and, rising, walked to John, who had remained in the wagon.

"My ma is in the house," Gabby said.

John's eyebrow rose, he glanced over at the weather-beaten boards, and he sighed, swinging his feet over the side, and jumping down to land with a thump. He tethered the horses to a tree and led Gabby to the house.

They had arrived just as Ma was preparing supper, the smell assailing their nostrils as Gabby opened the door. A black stew pot hung in the fireplace, making the hot, close little house shrink further. Her mother stood at the fire, stirring the stew with a wooden spoon. A toddler straddled her hip and had a fistful of her mother's hair in its little hand, the other hand stuck firmly in its mouth.

In a moment of empathetic clarity, Gabby wondered how her mother had come to arrive at such an impasse in life. She was not old; she had had Gabby when she was sixteen. Her father had worked in various jobs, the latest one on the railroad they had just traveled, but employment had dropped as the foreigners arrived. The Chinese were willing to do much more and work longer hours for much less, driving their American counterparts out of work.

"Who might you be then?" her mother asked. Her voice was shrill with surprise as they entered the house.

"I'm John Hawthorne, ma'am. I'm very happy to make your acquaintance."

Her mother stood by the fire, her mouth open, the soup spoon dripping onto the wood, and Gabby felt a hysterical giggle threatening to erupt. She stepped to the woman, relieved her of the child fastened at her hip, and she sat down at the wooden table to distract the young one.

John had stepped to her mother and gave a little bow. "So happy to meet you," he said again and motioned to her to join Gabby at the table. She did so, seeming to be automated in her stupefaction. The other children crept around them, surrounding the table and the stranger like little goblins coming in from the dark.

"I would like to tell you a little of myself, if I may." He bowed his head to her, inviting her audience, but she made no acknowledgment of his request and sat motionless, her hands in her lap.

John appeared at ease and continued to speak as if she had made the most gracious reply. "I have become acquainted with your daughter, Gabby, on the train ride from San Francisco. I was most impressed with her and can only think how divine your upbringing was to produce such an angel of grace and beauty. I come with the best intentions to request your daughter's hand in marriage. I can most certainly ask your husband if he is also about?"

As John spoke, Gabby's mom's convenience had ranged from unbelievability to scorn and then acquisitiveness as she looked at the material of his shirt and boots.

"He's not about, and he's not my husband," she said, her tone forbidding further questions, as she threw a glance at Gabby. Gabby's gaze dropped to her hands. She knew where he was – drinking away what little money they had. Many nights she had had to go and find her father slumped over a bar stool, or worse, when he had drunk too much, out on the street where the barkeep had tossed him. She felt the tell-tale redness enter her cheeks and John's gaze upon her. How she wished they could have begun their journey without returning to her home.

Her mother had other ideas. "Well... you know, Gabby is quite a help to me. Why we spent good money sending her out to my mother's to help her in her time of need. Speaking of which, girl, where's my money?" Her greedy hand snuck out and pinched Gabby on the arm, leaving a red, inflamed mark on her skin, and Gabby gasped holding her arm.

John stood, his chair crashing back on the floor, sending the little ones scampering out of the way with frightened yowls.

"Now see here, Mr. Fancy Pants, you don't get to come in here and upset me and the little uns," her mother said waspishly. Her eyes had narrowed, becoming little black orbs in the darkness of the little house. Gabby felt sick with repugnance and embarrassment.

"I came here to ask for your daughter's hand. Now I see that was a waste of time. It would be a blessing to remove her from this... " He waved his hand about. "From this loving home you've created," he said sarcastically.

She had also stood, her hand splayed on the table's etched wooden surface. Her fingers were calloused and split from dryness from the lye soap they used. Fingers that seldomly showed affection but often sharp stings of pain. Gabby found herself standing as well, with no memory of the movement, and she lifted her purse from her skirt with her grandmother's money.

"Here it is," she said. She wanted out. Out of this life.

She watched the snakelike movement of mother's hands as they grabbed the money purse, and then she turned her attention to John.

"If I let you have my Gabby, I lose a good worker. Someone who can cook and clean and take care of the little uns. I need something for my trouble."

Gabby felt her stomach heave with bile. The long, hot day and the tension as they rode to her home made her feel as if she would faint.

John's voice cut across the little room. Hard and cold.

"How much?"

A sly, sick look passed over her mother's face, and Gabby felt a loss she didn't know existed pass over her. An aloneness. An ache.

"I could let her go for, let's say... a hundred dollars," her mother said.

John withdrew his large wallet, and Gabby saw her mother's eyes widen as she licked her lips. Her tongue was long and pink, twining about before disappearing into that orifice.

John opened his wallet, threw two hundred dollars on the table, and reached across the table for Gabby.

***

The next day began with an impromptu wedding with the justice of the peace. John had given her a firm kiss on the mouth, which smelled of sweat and coffee. When they left the courthouse, she had pleaded with him for a picture to remember this day. He had acquiesced with a smile of indulgence, plucked some wildflowers from the courthouse grounds, placed them in her bonnet, and told her she was beautiful.

They met the others at the boarding house all sitting like improbable mushrooms with their conical hats under the trees. Today was a bit cooler but still steaming under the direct sun. It made no difference to the children who did as all children do: they played. They had found a roundish stone and were kicking it around the trees and the adults, and while Gabby could not understand the game's premise, she enjoyed watching them. She felt another wave of guilt pass over her at the thought of leaving her brothers and sisters behind, but it strengthened her resolve to ask John when they were settled if they might be sent for.

"Bao!" John called. The Chinese man rose to his feet and hurried over to John, his loose pants flapping as he moved.

"Is everyone ready to leave?" he asked the man. Bao nodded his head. "Yes, sir."

"All right, then." He stepped to the group and addressed them. "We'll be walking over to the livery where oxen, wagons, and supplies are ready for me. This will be a long journey... probably a month or more. If any women and children want to stay behind, I'll give you a dollar each." He motioned to Bao. "Tell them, and tell them they must learn English. There will be no more Chinese."

Bao nodded his head and began to speak. Gabby watched their faces, and when the women's expressions crinkled, and their mouths pursed, she knew he was giving them John's offer. One after the other, the women shook their heads, preferring to come with them than begin life anew in a strange country without their countrymen about them.

A cloud passed over the sun, and suddenly, Gabby felt a shudder ripple through her. They were all dependent on one man's charity and dream as they headed into the wilderness. Gabby knew without a doubt he would allow nothing and no one to slow him on his journey. She would need to keep up with whatever pace he set to show him how valuable she could be. She knew his frustration with the women and children and could help him manage that group; show the women their way of cooking and caring for the men, and keep the children out of the way.

They set off with eight wagons and sixteen oxen. Gabby had never seen such quantities of foodstuffs in one place before. Barrels of molasses, dried corn and fruits, beans, rice, coffee, tools, and canvas tents, the list went on.

He commanded Bao to bring all of the luggage they had brought with them from home and lay it at his feet. He had scoured it, discarding much of it but laying aside items he thought he could sell on the way or keep for himself. Teapots and small cups were taken, embroidered blankets and tunics were confiscated, and even the children's toys were culled.

Gabby's face was on fire as she watched her new husband exploit his employees. She watched them, watching John, wondering what thoughts might be going through their heads: anger, surely; frustration and resentment, certainly. Perhaps she could smooth things over with the women, indicating it was for the best. Fewer things meant lighter loads for the oxen, which might mean the children could ride instead of walk.

Yes, that is the tact she would take. So deciding, she approached John, who had carelessly let the discarded items fall onto the ground.

She touched his shoulder. "John," she said quietly. He twitched at her touch as if to indicate he had no time for her. "John!" she repeated a little louder, and he turned and looked at her. His eyes were cold and narrow, impatience radiating from his tight mouth.

"What do you need, Gabb? I'm busy... or perhaps you don't see that?"

She felt a pinch in her nose and strove to keep her voice even. "I'm sorry, John, for the interruption, but I was thinking with the lighter load, maybe the youngest of the children could ride?"

"Well, you were thinking wrong, then. They'll all walk, or they'll be left." He finished looting the luggage and took up a bag he kept for personal use.

"Bao!" he called. Bao appeared by his side. "Take this pile and pack it up. We'll sell it on the way. The rest, leave." He strode away, his boots, again, thumping the ground, punishing the earth as he walked.

Gabby and Bao stood by the discarded items. There were books, dishes, and treasures of family life. She felt sick to witness such cruelty and raised her eyes to meet simmering anger in Bao's.

***

They walked for miles that day, John constantly consulting his notebooks to ensure they were going in the correct direction. No one rode; the men carried the little ones in a back sling. They slept, and they cried. John refused to stop until he had made certain outposts.

Eventually, the nightmarish day ended, and Gabby dragged herself to begin the evening meal. They had consumed the noon meal as they walked; John would give no quarter.

Her back was aching as they set up pots of beans and bacon. She became acquainted with some of the women. Bin, Bao's wife, was most helpful, and they exchanged a few words of English. Gabby intended to teach them words and phrases so that John would be more favorably disposed to them when they arrived in the Dakota Territory.

The meal was eaten, as shots of gold, reds, and purples enveloped the sky, making Gabby feel hopeful that good things might be on the way. The children had fallen fast asleep, she was relieved to note. They were beautiful creatures. Some had burnished red cheeks from the sun, but their porcelain complexions were like ivory in the setting sun. Eyelashes lay like black feathers, their eyebrows perfect arches, each hair clearly seen on their white skin as if painted by a master artist. Such innocence and frailty.

"Gabby!" She heard John call and felt sick with nerves. This night was their wedding night. She knew how babies were made but had, up until now, kept herself for the imagined bliss a young girl would have. She squared her shoulders. She had chosen this life. She had chosen this man. She would sway him with her tender ways to treat the Chinese with compassion.

She entered their canvas tent and saw he had made up their cots. He was shirtless and stood for a moment gazing at her with the expressions she had seen on the cafe men in San Francisco.

He reached for her and began to undo the buttons of her shirtwaist.

"I'm sorry we aren't having our wedded bliss in a proper room, but soon, we will have a beautiful house that no one will take away from me." He turned and picked up a pile of silk. "I have a present for you my dear." He handed her the cool material, and she held it in her arms.

Holding the fabric by the edges, she let the rest fall to the floor. It was a beautifully made Chinese blanket; dragons writhing, and cherry blossoms sprouting across its silken surface.

Chapter 20

Gabriel had paused to take a drink from her teacup, her voice raspy and dry. She set the cup back in its saucer with a soft clink. Her napkin lay on her lap, and she brought it to her lips, the delicate lace fluttering as she touched it to her mouth. She rose from the table and took bread from a wooden bread box. Picking up the toasting rack, she set it over the fire, and soon, the smell of cooking bread filled the room.

"They must have made it to the Dakota Territory," I said, as I watched her turn the toast so the other side would brown. She stood before the fire, monitoring the bread, and then, deciding it was done, she brought it to the table with jam.

"Yes," she said, sitting down. She passed me the jam, and I spread it on my toast. "It was a difficult journey, but they all made it more or less safely. There was some sickness and a few injuries," she said to my unspoken question.

"Once they arrived, the hard work really began. According to his journals, he had already paid for land and set his claim. He had brought building materials in the wagons and had more delivered to his land in preparation of his arrival."

She appeared lost in thought. "Can you imagine what it must have been like for them? The journey was perhaps harder, but then at the end of their travels, still living in tents, the backbreaking work of raising a house, the language barrier, poisonous snakes and bears. It would try the most stable of minds."

"How did John know where to build his house so that it was over his mine?" I asked.

"He had purchased a vast swath of land, bigger than anyone had imagined..."

***

Gabby leaned over to spit on the ground. Her mouth was full of dust and dirt, kicked up from the workers as they felled trees. The grit crunched between her teeth. The sound of sawing and grunting surrounded her as they attacked the trunks. It was the women's work to remove branches, and she and the others' hands seemed permanently sticky from the sap, which proved impossible to remove. Even now, after scrubbing in preparation for the noon meal, her hands stuck to the bread and the cloths she had wrapped them in. She sighed, tucked her hair back in the threadbare bonnet, and winced as the sap was transferred to strands of hair, causing it to stick to the material. The bonnet she once wore on the train she had been so ashamed of was now a ghost of a memory. It was so battered and filthy it was hard to believe it had once been yellow.

She sighed again as she heard John's voice carrying over the sawing, yelling at the workers. He had found his mine, which had been a revelation. She had never seen him so happy, so young and excited. In those moments, she remembered her happiness on the train when he had been so full of hope and stories of his gold.

He had lifted her off her feet, swinging her in the air. "Gabby! Look what I've found!" he said. He set her down and pulled a bottle from his pants. It was a clear glass bottle topped with a cork, and he held it up to the sunlight and peered through the glass as he gently rocked it back and forth. She watched him, not even caring what was in the bottle, reveling in this joy. The sweat trickled down his forehead to his jawline, and she watched the muscle feather in his cheek. He parted his lips, little huffs of excitement coming from his throat. At long last, she turned to the subject of his interest and felt a shiver of excitement course through her. Beautiful, thin flakes of gold shimmered in the sun's rays. She watched as they twirled and swung in the water. So little could mean so much to one man.

"Oh, John! You've done it! You've found gold!" The workers cheered, and the children raced around, clapping their hands, not understanding the reason for their delight but feeling the happiness. The relief. The assurance of good things to come.

The cave John and the others had discovered was a series of caverns with one narrow opening thus far. The flakes in John's bottle indicated greater treasures upstream in the tunnels. He and the others scoured the caves, making elaborate maps and marking the walls.

Gabby remembered clearly the day John's dream had been realized. He had lifted the flap to their tent and sunk heavily onto the cot. He was panting from the work, and he stank. He had let his stubble grow into a great beard that was constantly encrusted with cave dust. His once linen shirt was dark brown, and she had given up washing it.

"What is it?" Her voice had been high with anxiety. There had been injuries, and she had been called upon to doctor them. So far, they had not been beyond her healing powers, but she lived in fear of when there would be an injury so grievous she could not help, and her patient would die.

"I've found it, darling, the light of my life. I've found it." He held out his hand, and five irregularly shaped nuggets sat in his palm. They did not shine like the flakes he had once been so proud of. These were burnished gold like the late setting sun.

"John..." she breathed. She stepped closer to view them, and his hand began to shake, fingers closing over the gold.

"We'll build our house over the cave. No one will take it from me."

***

Days of joy followed, days of wine and roses... if only in her mind. John hired more Chinese workers from Deadwood, and they came by the wagonfuls, all eager for work. Deadwood had become a small Chinatown with laundries, restaurants, and other entrepreneurial enterprises. John had to pay more for these new workers, which he bemoaned in great detail. But even he became content as his workers discovered more gold, and he hastened the building of the house. Work continued day and night, with different shifts every twelve hours. He worked constantly and slept near the sight, guarding the house and the mine. Bao tasked the Chinese women with preparing meals and fetching things for the men; even hammering was soon allotted to them. John did not like seeing Gabby performing menial tasks, and she soon found joy in taking care of the children, her younger brothers and sisters never far from her mind. She pictured them in that hovel of a house with Ma yelling, the dirty children scrapping for little bits of food, the latest man in their lives gone or drunk. She often wondered why her mother didn't go to California and help her grandmother with the cafe. There would be wages and a place to stay, and the little ones would have food and beds. Perhaps her grandmother couldn't take on so many, the children and the men that revolved around her mother's life, leaving mementos. As soon as John and the others built the house, she would press upon him the need to help her family.

Gabby had become acquainted with the Chinese women. Jin, Bao's wife, was especially open to the young woman. They had a boy child by the name of Bi. Bi had attained a little color to his creamy white skin, and his black eyes snapped. Gabby could see Jin and Bao's pride when they looked upon their son. There were five little boys in all, with one girl; a beautiful child that did not lose her white skin while playing in the sun. Her long and curved lashes gave her an almost cat-eye appearance, her lips were a little rosebud, and she smiled as easily as she cried.

There were four women in all, and from what Gabby could glean, they were from the same area in China and had worked as wheat and rice farmers, but the economy was poor in China due to wars with the Muslims, corruption, and other things. The group had pooled their money and purchased passage to America, hoping for a better life. Gabby had asked Jin if they had ever planned to return to China to farm, and she had shaken her head no. There would be no way to return. Their life, as it was now, was for survival.

Gabby had been charged with doctoring their group, which had increased since they had begun work on the house. Mental health care was non-existent in the 1800s, but it was apparent to Gabby that one of the women suffered from melancholia. She did her best to engage the woman, bringing her the savory bits of meat and the juiciest fruit when available.

"Jin, what's wrong with Yue?" Gabby asked.

Jin looked at the woman; her face losing its animation, and her eyes narrowing.

"I'm sorry," Gabby said. "It's not of my business, I'm sure. She just seems so... so lost."

"Yue is only one without child," Jin said. Her voice was soft, and Gabby leaned in to hear her words. "She did have child." She stopped speaking, and her eyes sought out her son, who was helping the men by handing them nails. Gabby could see a flash of pride quickly disappearing as she gazed at Yue.

"Did something happen to the child? Was it sick?" Gabby asked. Her heart broke for the woman. She knew what it was like to nurse babies and young ones through all manner of illnesses.

Jin shook her head. "Not sick. Girl," she said. Gabby's forehead puckered, and she looked at Jin. "I don't understand. Girl?"

"Yue have girl-child. Not boy."

"Where is the girl?" I asked.

Jin shrugged her shoulders. "Gone."

***

Later that night, Gabby questioned John about Yue's girl child.

"Leave it, Gabby," he said. He was pulling off his shirt, and she had prepared a bucket of water to remove the day's dust. He sat down on the cot and kicked a foot up, and she knelt, pulling at the boot, which came loose with a sudden movement.

"Yue seems very sad. I would like to do something for her, if I can," she said.

"I said leave it!"

"But John—"

"Gabby! The Chinese do not wish for girl babies. They are either left to to die or drowned. They do not bring honor to them, only financial hardship. Does that satisfy your curiosity?"

Gabby sat back on the hard ground. Her throat was thick with shock, and nausea threatened to upend her stomach contents. Even in her darkest days of taking care of the young ones at home, she had never wished harm on them.

"But what of the little girl we have here?" she pressed. "Why did they not kill her?"

"That family had more money, a larger farm. She is the only child they have had. Enough. I work with them all day and refuse to give them thought at night." He was angry at her for pushing him, and he slammed his boots back on and stood. "I'll sleep at the house."

She watched him go, berating herself for driving him away. She must be supportive, malleable, ladylike.

As she watched the tent flap waving in the night breeze, she felt a trickle of something. A feeling of irritation? Anger? She was beholden to him, but why must he treat her like a child? Why was she forced as a woman to be reliant on a man? Why would mothers murder their children? Surely, they did not want to. What monstrous societies allowed these things to happen?

She would befriend Yue and all of the women. Help them as much as she could.

She stood at the tent's opening. The coolness of the night was a balm to her sweating forehead. She could see the Chinese sitting about their campfires, talking in low tones, in Mandarin if her hearing served her right. They all knew of John's "no Chinese" decree, but she often heard them speak it while he wasn't about. She understood their need to keep their way of life present, their language, religion, and beliefs. She would never sanction murder and could not, would not, understand the need to commit such an act over something as simple as the sex of a child.

She gazed at the hills, rocky and black hills juxtaposed against the deep blue of the sky, the evergreens making black feathery brush strokes on the horizon. She felt ill at ease. Uneasy with John's continued absence, uneasy with a culture so different from hers. She heard an owl hoot in the trees and looked to where it might be. She could see it, bobbing its head, watching for its next prey. She started as it turned her way, its great yellow eyes studying her as if she were a rodent trying to hide in the rocks. She shuddered and dropped the canvas flap.

Chapter 21

Gabby rose the next morning to bird songs and the sounds of the workmen. She could not hear the sound of the women and children, and she wondered at that as she hurried out of the tent. The house was nearing completion and she was so eager to move in and leave the insects and the grime behind. Bao, Jin, and their child would move into the house and reside on the third floor, and the rest of the workers would build small one-room homes with leftover materials from the house. They would have to work fast before autumn came.

She walked to where the women were cooking over pots, making the interminable beans and bacon.

"Good morning, ladies," Gabby said. She reached for a long-handled stirring spoon and began to fill bowls, while the somber faced children placed them on wooden planks set on tree stumps.

The men were silent as they arrived from the house, with none of the usual Mandarin chatter when John was not around.

Gabby stepped to where Jin stood watching the children.

"Jin, is everything all right?" Gabby asked, brushing away the flies that had already found her.

Jin looked at her, worry in her eyes and her mouth downturned. She considered Jin a friend and shortly they would be living under the same roof.

"Please, Jin. Has something happened?" Gabby pressed her.

"Some men, they left," Jin said. Jin's English had improved remarkably but she still had problems communicating ideas and words.

"The men left? Where they getting supplies from Deadwood?"

Jin shook her head. "No, we have supplies." She pointed to where stacks of materials lay, ready to be used.

Gabby nodded. "The men left?" she questioned again.

"Yes, they no come back," Jin said.

"What?" Gabby was horrified. The house would not get finished and what of John's mine?

"Why?" she demanded.

"They are afraid," Jin replied.

"Afraid of what? Did John do something? Say something to scare them off?"

"No, not John. Down in the rocks." Jin would not elaborate and more workers were coming for their meal. There were definitely fewer men today. Gabby left the group and went in search of John.

***

Gabby reached the house, breathless from her run. She couldn't imagine how upset and angry John must be at the desertion of his workers.

She paused before the structure. It was truly becoming a home; her home. A place where she would live for the rest of her days. The veranda style porch wrapped the front of the house and rose to the second floor where a balcony was being constructed. The third-floor windows sparkled with the early sunlight as they protruded from the rooms. It was a sight to behold. She had never imagined that she, Gabby would ever live in such a grand house.

She stepped up the wide plank stairs, her fingers trailing the balustrade, imagining herself wearing a clean gown, coming in from the garden with a basket of flowers she had picked from the flower garden she would grow. She was brought to the present by John's voice, calling out from inside the house.

"You're a bunch of superstitious fools! I will not pay if you do not stay and work. I'll make sure you don't work anywhere around here. Get back down there and do not come up until I say, damn you!" Gabby froze in the hallway. She could see his outline black against the door in the back of the house. He was standing before a doorway under the stairs, screaming at the men. He was bent over, peering down at them, hawkish, his nose elongated by the shadow, his arms outstretched as he hammered them with his voice.

She would return later. She turned to walk quietly out of the house and she could feel his gaze upon her, not unlike the owl from last night waiting on its prey.

"Gabby!" She froze. "Get over here!" She turned, her heart hammering and humiliation turning her face a dirty red. Why must he speak to her so?

"You know what these coolies think?" He didn't give her time to formulate a thought, much less an answer. "These *men*, think there is a demon in the caves."

Gabby's mouth hung open, as John stomped toward her, his feet smacking the newly laid boards. "Did the women say anything to you?" he demanded. "Well?" He grabbed her by the upper arms and shook her so that her bonnet became askew and her hair tumbled down over her shoulders.

"John!" Gabby cried. "I don't know anything... I haven't heard anything!" He looked at her, searching her face, as she strove to smooth her expression. Jin mentioned the men had left, not why they had left, and there was little point in mentioning it to him now.

"Damn it!" He strode back to the doorway under the staircase and stared morosely down the wooden steps. Gabby could hear the men calling out to each other. A strange, musty smell wafted up from the shaft, making her want to choke.

He turned to look at her. "Get out! You're of no use to me." She turned back to the front door and stumbled out.

Chapter 22

"John was a real bastard wasn't he?" I said. She nodded, looking at her hands folded on the table. "All of this," I spread my hands out to encompass the house, the weather, her, "is a bad dream. A horror show. I don't understand any of it – least of all you." I felt my throat tighten and my breath quicken. "I don't understand why you stay. I don't understand how you know so much about Hawthorne. You say you read his journals and studied his account books; you're identifying with them. Gabriel, Gabby... is your real name even Gabriel, or is it something that you acquired as you stayed here? It isn't healthy for you here. I don't know what's in the caves; John, children, a demon for God's sake, but I think we need to leave. We should try to make it to the road. We can bundle up and I'll find something to pull you on." My voice had a sharp, high edge to it, and still, she sat there staring at her damn hands.

"Gabriel, listen to me!" I cried. "You need to come with me now. I'm going now, with or without you!" Not a movement, not a whisper of speech, nothing. I slammed my fists on the table and rose, heading to the hallway and taking my coat from the peg, as I donned mittens and my red scarf wrapping it tightly about my head.

"Last chance, Gabriel!" Silence answered me. Suddenly, I noticed the door under the stairs creeping open. *Damn it to hell,* I thought, as I walked over to it and kicked it shut. It held for an instant and then slowly began opening, the sick scent of decay drifting over to me, choking me. I turned my back on it. *Let it come*, I thought, and walked over to the front door, yanking it open.

The full force of the storm hit me, and I staggered back; it stole my breath, and I found myself gasping for air. *I will not stay here,* I thought. *Not in this house. Not with John.* I pushed through the drift that ran perpendicular to the door, as snow and icy crystals pelted my face, stinging my eyes and blinding me. I tried to shut the door behind me, but it was impossible. I propelled myself forward, searching for my truck. It resembled a large stone up ahead, *a tombstone,* I thought hysterically. I tried to remember how far it was to the main road. Surely, I could do it. I had lost count of the days I had been at Hawthorne House; they had melded into one dark, vile dream, like a waxed candle that had burned down to its wick, the wax dripping onto the table, eventually landing on a dirty floor.

The snow was gray, like greasy dirt that washed up on the roadways. I passed the truck, my knees on level with the bed of it, the icy snow forming a thick crust keeping me aloft. I trudged through the drifts, the pines that lined the road the only point of contact keeping me in line. It was getting darker as I moved further from the house. The cold was paralyzing, and my fingers and toes felt numb. Shadows crept across the snow, seeping into the surface, making me believe there were crevices when there were not; chasms were there were none. My lungs began to hurt as I inhaled the frigid air. My scarf was encrusted with ice and scraped along my frozen cheeks, and I began to feel a warmth and wondered if it was blood.

It was folly to come to Hawthorne House, and now it was folly to leave.

I continued to struggle, to walk in the storm. I felt a lightening to the air and brushed at my eyes. Was I seeing the road? Perhaps a snowblower? I stumbled faster, hoping to catch the driver. Praying they would see me in time and stop. Take me away from this nightmare. Take me to warmth and comfort. I felt my nose prickle and wondered if I could cry in this extreme cold. The tears would freeze in my eyes, and I would see the world through blurry vision like the bubbled panes of glass in Hawthorne House. Closer now. The light was brighter, and I could hear ragged breathing and realized with a rush of adrenalin it was me. I was almost there. A wave of snow passed before me, encircling me and cutting off my vision.

It cleared, and heartbreakingly, I found myself at the kitchen window of Hawthorne House; the weak light I thought guided me to salvation was Gabriel's candles. I had become lost in the storm. Got turned around. I wanted to cry out with frustration, but the frigid air had frozen my throat.

I crept to the window, my feet frozen blocks of ice. Her hands still lay folded on the table, white shards of ivory. Her hair was ragged, the white stringy wisps hanging to her shoulders.

She turned to me as I stared in shock... any flesh and mortal remains were gone.

Chapter 23

I felt the familiar tingling in my hands and feet. I was lying on a hard surface; cool air touching my face like inquisitive fingers. My eyes began to open, my sight bleary and unfocused. A face swam in front of me, the mouth moving, but no sound waves, no vibrations transmitted to my ear drums. I was floating along a sea of snow, brushing over drifts, encircling trees, landing on—

"Rachael!" Gabriel's face came sharply into focus. I could see every line, every pore. Her eyes were bloodshot and watery, and her thin lips trembled, wrinkling at the corners. Her short hair was tucked behind her ears. Her hair—

The memories slammed into place, and I sat up, pushing myself away from her.

"Stay away!" I cried. "You're not right—"

"Rachael, Rachael, hush... everything is going to be all right," she said. She held out her hands, her palms facing me, intending to reassure me, but I felt no comfort. I felt I might go mad as rushes of panic went through my body. I couldn't breathe. My throat had closed. I was going to lose my mind.

"You-you're Gabby, aren't you? What are you? A-a ghost? Are you what the Chinese were afraid of? Are you the demon?"

"No, Rachael. I am the caretaker. Please, child, stand up. Come with me. I think my time here is coming to a close." She turned from me and walked into the parlor, pausing at the door to look back at me. I was still sitting on the floor. My fear and mistrust kept me paralyzed. I didn't understand how I had gotten turned around in the storm. *Did all roads lead back to Hawthorne House?* I thought. *God help me, will I never escape?*

I rolled over to my hands and knees and slowly stood, as she waited patiently, a little old lady. She seemed so harmless in her dresses and low-heeled shoes. Someone who liked to garden and drink tea. To meet with other old ladies to discuss books and plants.

She turned to go into the room, and I followed.

***

We sat in our chairs. She seemed ill at ease. I was tense, remembering the horror from the kitchen window.

"Yes, I am Gabby." Her voice was a mere whisper, and in spite of myself, I leaned forward to hear her.

***

The Chinese had become terrified of the mines. They said it was Daolaogui, a demon of the mountains.

"Jin, is this true?" Gabby asked. Her breath came fast. John's dreams were so close to being fully realized, and now to have mining stalled because of a superstition. Jin would not look at her, and a feeling of incredulity overwhelmed Gabby.

"Jin, look at me!" Jin slowly raised her eyes to meet Gabby's. "Tell me! What are the men saying?"

"They say they see and smell the demon in the mines. It lives in the rocks where it is cold and damp." Jin's voice was low, full of belief.

"Jin! You can't possibly believe such a story. It isn't Christian. Surely you must know this!"

"It is a demon Mrs. Hawthorne. It shoot poison darts, and men can die," Jin said. Gabby felt her stomach lurch at this. She knew this could not be true. There were no demons in the mine. No poison darts. She looked at Jin and the other women who stood within hearing.

"You all know this isn't true! Can't you talk with the men? Make them understand this?" Gabby felt desperate to repair the damage, to get the men back to work, to make John happy.

They stared at her. They were not angry or belligerent; they were terrified, and Gabby felt the enormity of their belief. How do you reason with fear that has been instilled in you since birth? Each generation is reinforced with ideas of social unity and purpose in life – an avenue to control people.

But, their fear of the demon was greater than their fear of John.

***

The Hawthornes and Bao's family moved into the house a few days later, but Bao and Jin were visibly afraid and asked if they might join the others in making homes. The men discussed this away from the women's company, and when they came back, Bao's eye was blackened, and his lip was split. No further protestations were made.

Gabby was infuriated that John would treat a worker so and voiced it to her husband. His reply had devasted her.

"He's bought and paid for. Just like you. Don't ever question my judgment again."

Work continued on the mine with only the original men left. The days were endless. They chiseled rock, and the pick axes could be heard in every room of the house. Buckets of rock were filled, and men lifted them up the stairs to be taken by the women, who dumped them into a ravine a distance away. The children did not play their games but sat outside listless, watching the endless procession of women and buckets walk by.

Gabby attempted to play with the children, reading to them, teaching them nursery rhymes, but they would fall silent as their mothers walked by, sweat and dirt streaming down their faces, wearing expressions of misery and distress at the backbreaking work. The children would nestle close to Gabby, and she would wipe their tears. They would take long walks until the evening came, and she knew the mothers would be sitting at the outside table, too exhausted to move. Under all this agony, John's voice would rumble low and angry if one did not move fast enough, or if gold had not been found in more abundance. The wide vein of gold they had discovered, and continued to follow, had become shallow. Other tunnels were started, and noxious gases would pour out of air pockets long trapped in the mountains. Gabby could see the fear the Chinese held for their demon. She had learned through much prodding of Jin that the demon Daolaogui was a rumbling demon. His sounds were like thunder in the heavens, and he could destroy men with a single poisoned dart, causing the flesh to swell... and if it were not cut off, the victim would die within one day. Gabby would think of this whenever the sky opened and thunder and lightning devoured the land. The isolation of John's claim, and the heightened awareness of the superstitions made her feel exposed and unprotected. John was no help as he pushed the workers to work longer hours and take greater risks in the mines. His feverish intensity had consumed him. He was not the man she thought he was, and she began to think of home. Perhaps she could visit her mother, and she began her plan to approach him with this request. She waited until Sunday when even he decreed a break was needed.

She had prepared a special supper of beef and vegetables from the latest shipment from Deadwood. She waited until he was seated and had drunk his first whiskey of the night. She could hear the workers below them still working, John feeling no need for them to observe the Sabbath. "They believe in demons, what use is it for them to worship and pray on Sundays?" he'd said.

"John," Gabby said. Her voice was light, almost wheedling, and she hated herself for that begging tone. She cleared her throat and tried again. "John," she said again, her tone firmer. He glanced up at her and then looked down. He was making his endless entries in his journals.

"Yes? What is it?" His voice was terse, his pencil scratching, scratching on his paper.

"I was wondering—"

A low rumble sounded in the house. *Another storm,* thought Gabby. She glanced out the window to see the blue of dusk and the sun's setting rays jetting over the mountains, but no clouds scattered the skies.

The rumble began to gather sound, began to gather speed. The sound became deafening, shaking the house. The dishes rattled off the shelves and fell, shattering to the floor. John sprang from his chair, sending it backward, and launched himself across the room to the stairway. He flung back the door, and it crashed into the wainscoting, leaving a dent in the unpolished wood. He disappeared down the staircase while Gabby sat frozen in her chair. Jin and the other women appeared in the hallway; their eyes wide with shock, their faces as white as the tablecloth that lay before her.

She ran to them, and they descended the twisted little stairs. The children were shrieking at being left upstairs.

Gabby reached the bottom and ran for the entrance to the cavern. Fine dirt choked her, and she began coughing, vaguely aware of the sounds of the others behind her. The hellish noise continued, and Gabby was reminded of the sounds of the trains as they rumbled on the track, crescendoing as they traveled through town.

"John!" she screamed. Each inhalation brought wrenching coughs, and she had scarcely enough breath to call for him again.

"John!"

He did not answer, but the splinter of wood came directly ahead of her in one of the new tunnels the men had carved out of the mountain. She approached it, tripping over unseen rocks and divets in the ground. She could see the light swinging. It was John, and he held a lantern above his head, fading in and out as the dust rose around him, and then, she heard a sound that froze her blood.

Screaming and groans, wild, primal shrieking came from a load of rocks blocking the tunnel's pathway. Gabby could hear cries in Mandarin, groans and weeping, as John stood before the cave-in. Sharp broken planks stood at odd angles like unformed teeth from the earth, as rubble continued to fall, wedging into the crevices of the large boulders. Softening the screams, plugging them as if they were sinking underwater, with little bubbles of sound making their way out into the dirty air until all had popped.

Gabby stood, her hands on the wall, feeling the grit from the dust under her palms, sweat creating a slimy feel, still coughing and choking on the arid dust.

John whirled to confront her, the lantern swinging out. "What the hell are you doing down here?" he demanded. He caught sight of the women behind her. "Get over here and help dig them out!"

The women rushed to the pile and began pulling at the stones, the rubble continuing to fall on their heads.

"John!" Gabby cried. "We need to get out of here. The rest of the cave is falling!" He stepped to her and slapped her. "Get the hell out of here!"

She stared at him, stunned, as blood filled her mouth. The women did not look back as they continued digging at the rubble, letting the ceiling rain down on them.

"John! We're all going to die down here."

He looked at her in the dusty gloom and then at the women on their knees, grabbing handfuls of dirt and rocks, crying and talking to the men in the hope they would hear them.

John drew in a breath and threw the lantern at the rock wall, sending flames snaking down the wall to the dirt floor. Gabby gasped, and the other women turned. She could see Jin's face in the firelight, dirty, tear-stained, hopeless.

"Come!" she screamed and pulled the women from the floor.

***

They assembled in the parlor. Their faces were blackened, and their clothes stained and torn. John sat in his chair, drinking whiskey sans glass. The women were in a state of shock, and the children leaned into them; their faces puzzled and tear-stained. They did not understand, could not understand what had just happened.

John cleared his throat and took another swig of alcohol. "Today was unfortunate, but it must not set us back."

Gabby stared at him. Her lip had dried shut but had opened again when she sipped water. He was out of his mind.

He continued, "Tomorrow, we will begin on the next set of caves I have mapped out for us." He rose, stepped to the sideboard, and retrieved one of his notebooks, and then sat down and opened it. "We will begin on the west tunnel. The women," he indicated the dirt-stained women, "will begin chopping through the rock, and the children can carry buckets up the stairs to the ravine. Of course, it will be slower going, but I trust we can work longer hours to make up the time."

"John—"

"I'll not hear one word from you. I am your husband and you will do as I say!"

"What is my task?" Gabby asked.

"You, wife, are to wash my shirts."

***

A living, breathing nightmare had begun. The women and children worked from dawn until dusk, chipping, moving dirt, carrying debris. By the end of the day, the children could barely move, and Gabby would help them by taking the buckets from the top of the stairs out to the ravine, allowing them to rest for a few precious minutes. John noticed but did not chastise or stop her. He had tied the children together, ankle to ankle, so they would not get lost in the mines. The eldest, a nine-year-old, led them back and forth, up and down in never-ending succession. Gabby asked for help, offered to go to

Deadwood to find more men to replace the women and children, and was met with anger and violence. The gold had run out, and John was getting desperate to shore up his accounts and pay loans he had taken from the bank to tide them over until more veins of gold were unearthed.

They had begun work on another tunnel. John had high hopes for this one due to a few flakes he had found in the early buckets he had panned. He tied the children as he always did, ankle to ankle, and they began the never ending succession of bucket carrying. They weren't children anymore. Their fathers had been killed; their childhoods vanished into the underground of the undergrounds. John's abuse left them with painted doll faces, no expressions. No hope.

Gabby watched them descend the stairs. "I'll be here when you come back up. I'll have water and the last of the dried fruit. Good, yes?" She tried to smile, but they made no indication they had heard her. She watched their little heads twist around the staircase as they descended, their buckets hitting the stone wall, clanking.

She could hear John yelling at the women, and then that, too, disappeared as he went further into the tunnel.

She waited by the stairs, glasses of water and strawberries ready to eat. The fruit was expensive and meant for John, but he was in the depths of the tunnels, and would not know.

She leaned against the opposite wall, watching the stairs, waiting for the children. How long could they go on like this? The women no longer talked to her or even looked at her. She could sense their helpless fury at the man who mistreated them and abused their children.

She walked over to the stairs and peered down; John would be furious if he caught her coming down to the tunnels. It appeared to offend his sensibilities on what a wife, his wife, should do. She could see nothing of their heads or hear the clink of the buckets, as she leaned her head against the door; a sick feeling of unease and exhaustion coming over her. She wondered if she might be ill; that would be unthinkable to John.

A thin shred of noise found its way up the stairs, a glimmer, a sliver, a high-pitched sound wafting up the staircase. She ceased to breathe as she bent down to hear. Had someone fallen? One of the children? There had been many falls as they learned to navigate the rocks and fragmentation of the floors.

Screams ripped through her body, and she almost fell down the twisting stairs as she rushed down to the tunnels. She entered the cavern at a dead run and stopped. The women were supposed to be in the new tunnel opposite the one where the men had been buried alive, but their voices were not coming from that direction. They were coming from one nearby that had not been fully explored yet. She ran to the entrance and saw Jin and the others on their knees; some were crying, and others were in a state of shock. John stood over them, wearing an expression she had never seen before. Shock and anger, perhaps guilt? He was never guilty of anything.

"John! What's happened?" she cried. Jin stood and took her arm, pulling her frantically to the others. "Our babies, our children, are in the shaft! Oh, help us, please! Please, Mr. Hawthorne." She had taken his arm, and he shook it off, sending her staggering.

"Weren't you watching them, John? They went down the wrong tunnel, and you didn't even notice?' He looked at her, equal amounts of fury and rage warring in his expression, and he shoved her, sending her reeling to the ground.

"We can get them out!" he yelled, picking up a lantern and striding to the shaft. Gabby could see the pile of arms and legs, their necks bent at impossible angles, the light catching the metal buckets as if they were buried in silver.

She stepped back and watched him, the lantern swinging on his arm, the bronze hair catching the light. Sweat and dirt made a muddy substance and that filled in the creases of his neck. She remembered when she first saw him all those months ago. How strong he had seemed, how happy she had been when he had whisked her away from her mother and her miserable life.

She stepped behind him and, with a gentle push, sent him over the edge.

Chapter 24

"You're protecting the children," I said.

"Yes," she replied. "I am the caretaker."

My head swiveled to the hallway as the door to the tunnels fell open. Sounds resonated from the stairs, echoes from one hundred years ago. Sweet sounds, child-like sounds. I sensed the warmth of little bodies and smelled the sweet scent of children. These little shades had their lives cut short, all lying at the bottom of a mine shaft with the demon John.

"Will you stay with us?"

"You're so pretty!"

"Will you protect us?"

I rose from my chair, terrified and impassioned by their pleas.

"Gabriel! Help me!" I cried.

"I'm sorry, child. It's really not up to me," she said. "My time is passing. I want to stay here with you and the little ones, but I feel myself fading. I cannot fight him anymore. He is a beast and must be kept down in his hole."

"No! I don't accept this. I'm leaving this house," I cried. I felt the children move around me. Their innocence so poignant, I wanted to cry. "I'm sorry," I said to them. "But I can't stay here with you. This isn't for me."

I felt a rumble through the floorboards. The pictures on the walls swayed, and the door under the stairs banged open, niching the wall as it did over one hundred years ago.

Gabriel grasped the arms of the chairs, struggling to rise. "John! Leave them alone!" she cried, but her voice was wavering, frailty overwhelming her.

I moved to help her and placed my arm around her. "Sit," I said. She made a move as if to stop me, and I gently held those paper thin hands and turned.

I ran for the stairs, the shades of the children racing beside me, almost falling at the twisting stairs, grabbing the greasy handrail to steady my flight.

I entered the cavern, the dusty motes choking me as I inhaled.

"Where are you, John!" I screamed. The children swirled about me, their mouths open in fright. I could feel their silent screams, their desperation as their cold little hands encircled mine, their diaphanous bodies pressed against me. It was like touching fog or morning mist.

He came. He came from the rocks; he came from the fissures and the chasms. His stinking, malicious presence filling the tunnels and cavern where I stood. The faltering light from the stairs winked in and out as he gravitated around us. Swirling movements, dizzying in their speed. I felt a sense of death and rage so complete, all hope and love of self and others was dead. He showed me horrible things. His loss and confusion at the putrid stink of his sick parents. The abuse at the hands of men as he begged in the sandy streets in the shadows of the mission. His shock and horror at the stabbing of Sam and his rage as he murdered Freddy. The guilt of the dead children, his frustration, and his wife's betrayal as he fell into the shaft to join their broken bodies.

"None of it matters now, John. Leave them alone!" I cried. A maelstrom of hate erupted around me. The clamors and shifting of the rocks around me sounded like a thousand freight cars careening out of control. I covered my ears, crying out, though I could not hear any sound from my vocal cords. The children huddled around me; the empty pits of their eyes elongated as if they were crying. They broke my heart, and I felt tears well up in my eyes as I tried to gather them around me, feeling for one incredible moment their warm little bodies, their shivers of terror and fright. Their aloneness. I would give my life for them in return for their freedom.

"Leave us, John!" I screamed. "You have no power. I will not leave them!"

Chapter 25

The sun burns through my eyelids. I wake in a dusty room; the blanket smells slightly of mold. Silence fills my ears. There are no shrieks from the wind, no howls, no ice hitting the windows. I sit up and run to the window. There is blessed, blessed sunshine everywhere. I feel my breath catch, and my vision blurs, just like the wavy panes of glass. I run from my room and rush down the stairs. The house is warm, and I cry out for Gabriel. I look in the kitchen and the parlor, run to the front door, and open it. The snow is undisturbed, with no signs of where I had broken through it to find the main road.

I look around, feeling unreality seep into me. Was this a dream or a nightmare? Had I hallucinated it? A product of almost freezing to death?

I run back up the stairs to check in Gabriel's room. There is no sign of life. The bed is made. I check the closets and dresser drawers. Nothing. I glance at the surface of the dresser, noting old daguerreotypes and lift one to study it. It is of a woman with flowers tucked into her bonnet and a man. The woman is smiling and I can almost feel her joy, but the man is frowning as if irritated with the photographer. My breath leaves me as I know for certain it is Gabriel.

A clunking sound comes from the hallway, and I turn to look. Running, I return to my room and cross the floor to look out the window.

Snowplows!

The beautiful sight of snow shoots into the trees, leaving the gravel uncovered. The trees bowing down under the weight of the ice. They reach my truck. I stand frozen at my window, and my heart sings with happiness, knowing rescue is at hand. I can leave this place and never return.

I step closer to the window and watch them scoop out my truck, throwing the snow over their shoulders with great shovels full. I need to go downstairs and let them know I am here, that I am all right, that I am so happy to see them, but I feel somehow rooted to the spot. I peer closer. Yes! They find my suitcase and moments later locate my laptop. I wonder if it is salvageable. No matter, I am sure work will replace it.

Wait.

I see something.

I feel my heart lurch.

They have uncovered a red scarf and mittened hands.

They have uncovered me.

The children, my shade children, envelope me.
I am the Caretaker.

Acknowledgments

Many thanks to my editor Stuart Budgen for his guidance and help. Special thanks to karen@coverKreations for designing my beautiful cover.

About the Author

The Caretaker is the third installment in my Haunted Historical Mystery Series where I endeavor to take my readers on a journey around the United States to be fascinated by our country's history in a set of chilling books that I hope you will love. Thank you for reading and please leave a review. My next book will be coming out in the summer of 2024, *The Haunting of York Hall*. Any questions or comments? Please visit my website at reginawixon.com. or follow me on Facebook where I will keep you updated on upcoming books. Questions? Please email me at regina.wixon@gmail.com – I'll be happy to hear from you!

Books by Regina Wixon

Haunting in the Louisiana Mists

Disappearance in Hockomock Swamp